MANDATORY REPAIRS

COLLIER'S CREEK

ELLE KEATON

ONE

Nash

"Yes." Nash Vigil nodded, gritting his teeth as he did so. "Yes, I do understand how patient you've been."

It was a good thing it was physically impossible to reach through phone lines. He desperately wanted to strangle the condescending faceless fucker who was calmly reminding Nash how they'd allowed Twisted Pine Ranch plenty of time to pay the monthly installment—with a hefty late fee added to the balance, of course. He swore under his breath, worried that one of his molars had given up the ghost.

Of course, Robin Simpson chose that very moment to stroll into the Twisted Pine kitchen. The owner of the ranch had been working out in one of the barns. She was bundled up against the October chill in a thigh-length barn coat that was older than she was and a hand-knit hot-pink cap pulled down over her ears. The hat made her look slightly impish. Or deranged. Nash wasn't sure which. Spotting him sitting at the desk, she slowed down. He directed a frenzied smile in her direction, even though it made his face hurt.

"What's going on?" she mouthed, not fooled by Nash's false enthusiasm. "Smoke's coming out your ears."

"Nothing," he mouthed back as he listened to the representative rattle off the new round of paperwork that needed to be filled out if they were going to miss or delay another payment.

"I'll send these to the email we have on file."

Nash certainly hoped they weren't sending it to another, different email. Perhaps one they'd made up just to be bastards.

Then they started in on how important it was to keep abreast of finances. Nash wanted to ask if they'd ever tried running a ranch. If they'd ever ridden a horse or been so isolated only satellite phones worked—and not reliably. He did not. Instead, he tuned out and focused on the game of spider solitaire he had going on the desktop computer in front of him.

Peeling off her fleece-lined jacket along with the hideous cap, Robin hung them together on a hook next to the kitchen door. Shooting him another questioning look, she toed off her boots and padded over to the sink where she began to fill the kettle.

"Coffee?" she asked.

Nash nodded as the rep droned on.

Finally, they got to the point. "You have fourteen business days to fill out the paperwork and get it back to the agency. We can't guarantee that Twisted Pine qualifies for the exemption," they said.

Of course they couldn't. Nash nodded. "Will do."

"It's been a pleasure speaking with you, Mr. Vigil. Is there anything else we can help you with today?"

Nash sincerely doubted it had been a pleasure. It certainly hadn't been a pleasure on his end.

What he really wanted to do was tell the rep it would be great if the loan servicing company would actually help the ranch by reworking their loan and lowering the crippling interest rate they were paying. But, apparently, that was "not something that could be considered at this time." Managing not to say what he was really thinking, Nash clicked off with a "no, thank you," and set the phone aside.

Saying anything negative to Robin about the loan was not an option. She was the one who'd taken out the predatory loan in a moment of panic a few years ago, after her mother had died. Ranch finances had been in the worst shape they'd been in since the recession in the 1980s—when Robin was a toddler and Nash hadn't been born yet—and the possibility of losing the ranch as well as her mother had made her reckless. Nash didn't blame Robin but did wish she'd reached out for help before signing on the dotted line.

"What was that?" Robin asked.

"Just talking to the loan servicing company again. My semiannual attempt to get them to rework the rate."

"I'm sorry, Nash."

Robin felt deeply guilty about the state of affairs, and Nash knew that, like him, she lost sleep worrying about their future. This was the only place Robin had ever lived and Nash had been at Twisted Pine since adolescence. This was their home. Nash couldn't imagine himself living anywhere else. The land under his feet had a grip on his soul like no other.

"One of these days when I call, they will have a different answer."

"Isn't that the definition of insanity?" she asked. "Doing the same thing over and over and expecting a different outcome?"

"Call me crazy, I guess," Nash said with a grin. "Want a cup of coffee?"

A few hours later, after visiting the horses and checking in on his not-so-secret project—goats—Nash drove the twenty miles into Collier's Creek. He wanted a beer and needed some downtime that didn't include the folks at Twisted Pine. As much as he enjoyed and appreciated his coworkers, sometimes a man just wanted to sit at a bar and brood.

When he rolled up to the first stop sign in town, he took a left, deciding to head to Randy's Rodeo Grill and Bar since they had barbecue and the best of the local beers. There was also plenty of parking, one of the benefits of a small town. Thankfully, there was no line dancing tonight.

Nash loved small-town rural life—with the exception of square dancing. The lack of suitable men was irritating too. He wasn't the only gay man in town by any means, but most of them seemed to have already found partners. There were a few outliers, but Nash wasn't interested in Logan or Coop. He'd known them too long. He knew the sheriff swung his way too, but he did *not* have a law enforcement kink.

Besides, Nash wasn't looking for love. He knew better. Love was just a way for someone to break your heart.

After pushing inside Randy's, Nash paused near the entrance. The tavern was warm, dimly lit, and smelled faintly of stale cigarette smoke, a ghost of times long past. Lucinda Williams played overhead, and Nash automatically started humming along with her.

The place wasn't jam-packed, but most of the tables were taken. Cooper Ellis, Will Evans, and a guy Nash didn't recognize right off the bat were playing pool in the back, the sound of the balls chinking against each other just audible over Lucinda's voice. But he wasn't there to shoot the shit with old friends; he was there to brood.

A spot opened at the bar, and he headed for it.

"This spot taken?" he asked the person sitting on the next stool over.

Nash didn't recognize him. Slowly, the stranger turned his head and took Nash in, down and back up, before meeting his gaze. He looked at him *hard.* A hunger glinted in his eyes that

Nash could all but feel brushing against his skin, and surprisingly he reciprocated it.

Yup, Coop and Logan were off the menu, but this silver fox fit the bill perfectly.

"Now it is," the stranger replied, his smile wide and welcoming.

Randy's was one of the more open-minded bars in town, but a guy still needed to be careful. Overall, Collier's Creek was more tolerant than it had been even ten years ago, but even so, this was no place for a stranger to feel comfortable picking up men.

Randy himself was behind the bar tonight. The man had to be almost seventy and complained constantly about arthritis and being on his feet all the time, but he still worked full time, probably more. He twitched an almost-smile in Nash's direction.

"Nash, we haven't seen you in a while. What can I pour you?"

"What's good?"

Randy glanced back at the taps as he pondered the question.

"CCB's new coffee porter is worth a pint."

Collier's Creek Brewery had been around a few years now and even won a medal or two in Denver. Plus, one of the ingredients was coffee. In Nash's opinion, there really wasn't a wrong way to go when coffee was involved.

"You should have one. I'm on my second," New Guy said, wobbling his glass back and forth and licking his lips as he did so.

"Alright then, I will."

A lifetime of living in a small town meant Nash knew better than to stare at strange men, and he was trying to keep his gawking to a minimum. But really? This silver fox was his catnip. His thick hair had a slight curl to it, and Nash briefly imagined himself running his fingers through it. Silver-white streaks threaded through darker strands, gleaming like crystal where the light landed on them and adding to the temptation.

Too bad the light was so low. Nash wanted to see him more clearly. What color were his eyes anyway?

And he needed not to be thinking those thoughts.

"Here ya go," Randy said, setting the porter in front of him. "How're things?"

Nash waggled his head and took a long gulp, emptying his glass a few inches. Everyone in town knew everyone else's business and it was an open secret that Twisted Pine was struggling and had been for years. They weren't the only ones, but it was a club Nash would rather not belong to.

"Meh," Nash admitted wryly. "We're not going anywhere yet. But damn, it seems like it gets harder and harder every day."

"How's the trip doing?" Randy asked with a grin. The bar owner knew Nash would rather talk about his newest project than anything else.

Nash couldn't help but smile, thinking of the goats he'd talked Robin into giving space to in one of the barns and one of the yards. New Guy—who also smelled *damn* good— leaned a little closer, almost brushing his shoulder.

"A trip? What's a trip? Other than the obvious—*a trip*," he asked. His words seemed a little blurry, making Nash wonder just how much the man had had to drink, but it also could have been his overactive imagination. Nah, he snorted. An overactive imagination was not something he suffered from.

"Trip's another name for a group of goats," Nash replied.

The stranger squinted at Nash, then at Randy, then back at Nash. Nash raised an eyebrow in response and sipped more of his beer as he tried not to laugh at the expression on the other guy's face. The beer was excellent.

"Ahhh." New Guy's brow furrowed. "But what's wrong with herd?" He downed the rest of his drink and waved his empty glass at Randy. "Can I get another one of these, please?" He asked Randy. "It's really hitting the spot."

Plucking a fresh glass from a tray behind the bar, Randy turned back to the taps, rinsed the glass out, and began filling it. However, the tap chose that moment to blow, forcing a bunch of foam into the glass that then shot back out and onto Randy's face. With an irritated sigh, Randy set it back down.

"Gotta change the damn keg," he informed them before heading toward the back room where Nash knew all the fresh kegs were stored.

"Well?" New Guy prompted, nudging Nash with his elbow and leaning in again. "Trip?"

Nash should hate that he was being pestered. He should be wary of this seemingly oblivious but handsome man sitting next to him. But he didn't mind the questions and alarm bells were not ringing. At least, not the right ones. Damn, it had been too long since he'd had sex with anything other than his hand—or even been attracted to someone. But no way was he picking up some stranger at Randy's, he told himself. The town gossips would find out within seconds, and Nash hated people knowing his business.

No offense to Randy.

"Uh." Nash forced himself to focus on the question. "Trip. Right. First of all, it's a more interesting word than herd."

Really, that was the only reason Nash needed.

"Yeah, duh." New Guy was watching Nash closely, a warmth to his eyes that Nash was unused to; it almost made him want to break his rules.

"And, um, it's very specific to goats. No other group of animals has that name. You know, like a murder of crows or a cauldron of bats. Supposedly, it comes from the Dutch word *trippen*, which means to skip or hop. I thought it was cool when I found out." He finished his short etymology lesson feeling a bit self-conscious. Surely, this guy was just feigning interest.

The man stared at him for so long that Nash started to wonder if he'd paid any attention at all to what Nash had said. Then, languidly, like the sun climbing up over the horizon on a winter day, a smile slowly formed on New Guy's lips.

Nash's cock twitched.

Down, boy. This one is not for you.

"That is so cool," the man whispered just as Randy set his beer in front of him. "That is definitely the best word ever. Hold it. You have goats?" he asked as if it was akin to owning a diamond mine. "Tell me about them. Do they have names?"

Halfway through his second beer and explaining his plans for the goats, Nash felt New Guy's warm hand land on his thigh.

"Uhhh," Nash stuttered to a stop. Granted, goats themselves were probably boring—although he wasn't sure boredom was worth a grope. And his plans weren't exciting either. Nash wanted to try his hand at making artisan cheeses, maybe soaps, and then maybe try selling them at the farmer's market. If they took off, it'd be another income source for the ranch.

And if they weren't successful, he'd see if Robin would open space in the barn during the summer tourist season for goat yoga. That was popular and hip, right? Maybe even locals would come out for classes.

"Um, that's my thigh you have your hand on."

"It's a nice thigh," New Guy said wistfully, squeezing Nash a little harder and rubbing the outside of Nash's leg with his thumb.

Nash rolled his eyes up to the ceiling. Only he would sit next to a stranger with roaming octopus hands. Gently, he pried the hand off his thigh, then immediately missed the heat of it. *Fucking hell*, he snorted at himself. He needed to make up his mind.

Luckily, Randy had wandered off to see if the guys playing pool wanted anything. He'd heard everything about the goats a multitude of times.

"You need to be more careful. Not everyone is... *er...* friendly."

Nash thought about joining the pool players but something about the man he was sitting next to kept him there. He felt somewhat protective of New Guy, which was ridiculous since he obviously had a few years on Nash. He'd survived this long, so he obviously wasn't an idiot.

"Yeah," the man finally said with a gusty sigh. "*I know*. Be careful. Follow the rules." He rocked his head back and forth. "That's what makes me tick. Tick tock, tick tock. Blah blah blah" The last head waggle included a giggle and had him nearly tipping over and falling against Nash's side.

Whoever he was, he needed a keeper. The irrational thought that the keeper should be him slunk into Nash's head. And once he'd thought it, he couldn't ignore it.

"How much have you had to drink?" Nash asked.

"Just enough." The guy leaned close again, and this time gravity won.

"Okay dokey, I think it's time to get you home," Nash stated as he righted his new friend and looked for Randy, who was still nowhere in sight.

Damn.

The guy perked up at Nash's words and unsuccessfully tried to balance himself. "Home? With you? I'm just staying"—he waved vaguely—"that way." Turning around, he squinted at the entrance. "Pretty sure. It's one way or the other."

Oh, for fuck's sake.

Standing up, Nash tossed a couple bills on the bar to cover his tab and enough for New Guy's if he hadn't paid already.

"Come on, let's get you home before you get in serious trouble."

Without arguing, the guy rose to his feet, swaying a bit before he began a shambling stumble toward the door. Catching up with him, Nash looped the other man's arm over his shoulders to keep him from falling over. At least, that's what he told himself. The fact that his body was tingling from wrist to shoulder meant nothing.

"Since I don't know where you're staying, I'll buy you a night at the Wagon Wheel."

Collier's Creek oldest motel was just around the corner from Randy's.

"Ssure... Waaagon Wheeeel. I like that. Did you ever play that game as a kid? Oregon... Oregon... something."

"Oregon Trail?"

"Yeah! That! I'm from there. Well, not there specifically, but kind of. That was a fun game until you died of cholera."

He sounded so sad about his character dying, Nash was almost moved to comfort him. Nash had been more of a Grand Theft Auto and Left4Dead kind of guy. Not that he'd had a lot of time to play those kinds of games when he was a kid. Or money.

Nash steered them around the next corner and the Wagon Wheel came into view. It was everything the name implied: kitschy, quaint, and basic. Nash knew the manager fairly well and was sure Kai would let the guy crash for the night as long as Nash footed the bill.

"I've never been this close to the sky." New Guy tried to spin in a circle but tripped and Nash grabbed at his arm before he hit the pavement. Collier's Creek was almost seven thousand feet above sea level, so the sky did feel very close here, as if a person only had to reach up a foot or two and you'd be able to run your fingers against the expanse of it. The sky was just one of the things Nash loved about his adopted hometown.

"Come on, Wonder Boy. Let's go talk to Kai."

Once he got Mr. No-Name settled—he wasn't asking for the guy's wallet and Kai was fine using Nash's card—Nash headed to the other side of town to grab a massive burger at The Peaks so he wouldn't be tempted to check in on the stranger later. Which was ridiculous. It's not like he knew this guy. He'd never see him again.

TWO

Max

What the hell had he done?

The question bobbed in the murky ether of Max's semiconsciousness, teasing him with its unanswerability.

He had no idea.

But he'd done something, that was certain.

His head ached and his tongue was bone dry.

Slept with his mouth open? Had a car accident? Got run over by a train? His body felt like he'd been hit repeatedly with metal pipes, but that seemed more metaphorical than a reality. Try as he could, he couldn't recall a car or a train, much less metal pipes.

He risked moving his head. A pathetic mewing sound escaped his lips, the minuscule vibration causing his skull to throb painfully. Instinctively, he smacked his lips together, trying to create moisture somewhere in his mouth.

Spoiler, it didn't work.

Keeping his eyes closed, he reached out blindly with one hand, feeling for the nightstand and the can of water he normally had sitting on it. He'd put one there yesterday, he was sure. The tips of his fingers encountered nothing. Reluctantly forcing himself closer to being fully awake, the pain in his head becoming more acute, Max scooted his body toward the edge of the mattress in search of water.

Still nothing.

That was when he realized the morning sounds were all wrong as well. They were not what he was used to hearing daily. His heart started to pound, which made his head hurt more. The rumble of big vehicles, semitrucks maybe, reached his ears instead of the squabble of seagulls and crows that gathered in the park across from his condo.

Crap.

He wasn't at home in his big, comfy bed. He'd sold the condo. All his belongings, including the nightstand, were currently in Cooper Springs with his brother. He also suspected he wasn't in the quaint room he'd rented at the Collier Creek Bed and Breakfast because it was nowhere near a highway.

Dread coursed through his veins now, a heady cocktail that forced him fully awake and out of the cocoon state—which, it turned out, had been muting just how incredibly awful he felt.

There was so much ibuprofen in his future.

This kind of thing did not happen to Maximillian Stone. Maybe to his twin brother, Xavier, but not to him. Max was the responsible one. Max didn't wake up in strange places with no memory of the night before. Hesitantly, he peeled one eye open, sensing that any significant amount of light could wreck him.

He had a limited sight range, but there were more hints that this room wasn't the one he'd rented at the Collier's Creek Bed and Breakfast. The hideous wagon trail mural on one wall was a big clue.

Surely, he would've remembered that.

Cracking his other eye open, Max lifted his aching head to peer around the room. The walls were covered by a mural telling a lurid tale about the Old West. All four colorful murals were an unfortunate 1950s portrayal of American history and made Max even dizzier, what with the suspiciously tidy white settlers who'd headed west to make their fortunes and the wildly inaccurate depiction of scowling Native Americans who already lived in the region.

What the hell?

Holy massive banana slug.

Where was he and what had he done? Max scoured his memory of the day before.

After a long-ass day of navigating roads that became smaller and smaller the closer he drew to his destination, Max had arrived in Collier's Creek in the late afternoon. He'd immediately checked in at the bed-and-breakfast and been given the tour by his chatty host, Delores Suarez.

Which was why he knew he wasn't there right now. The Collier's Creek Bed and Breakfast leaned hard into the cowboy culture—all stone fireplaces, brown leather furniture, and exposed ceiling beams—of the small town, not the poorly equipped and morally suspect Donner Party motif.

"Fucking hell. What happened?" he asked out loud.

Speaking made his already pounding head throb harder. Max hardly ever drank to excess. Had he gotten drunk? Then a more hideous and horrifying thought struck. Why was he in this strange room? Had he, in a drunken stupor, hooked up with someone?

At the age of forty-two?

A stranger, obviously, since he knew exactly no one in Collier's Creek. Ignoring his queasy stomach, he rolled onto his back and hastily threw the covers back.

Relief flooded through him when he realized he was wearing the jeans and white t-shirt he'd put on yesterday morning in Pocatello, Idaho. Not that he wouldn't have minded meeting a sexy someone and doing the horizontal tango, but he usually liked to remember the experience and get to know the person first.

Massaging his temples and face with both hands, Max forced his body to a sitting position. He desperately needed to hydrate.

Movement in the corner of his eye caught his attention. *Jesus Christ!* He almost screamed out loud at the sight of the unkempt man—*in the mirror, for fuck's sake*. His salt-and-pepper hair, more salt than pepper anymore, stood up every which way and massive dark circles had formed under his eyes. He had more baggage than SeaTac Airport's lost and found, which was saying a lot. He'd walked past there once during the holidays, and bags had been piled three and four high like a giant game of Jenga.

No one in their right mind would take him home. Crisis averted.

Ignoring his reflection, Max saw two glasses wrapped in wax paper below the mirror. He shuffled off the bed as fast as he dared toward the dresser. Maybe it would be faster if he just drank from the faucet?

What the holy hell had he done last night?

After gulping down two full glasses of water, he checked the time. Just past seven a.m. The hotel's shower beckoned. If he had to do the walk of shame, at least he would be clean. Stripping and draping his clothing across the tiny sink, Max stepped into the spray.

"Oh, god," he moaned as the water sprayed against his skin. The hot water running across his skull and over his sensitive skin felt incredible and terrible at the same time. Maybe he was coming down with something? He didn't think that was it; this felt distinctly like a hangover. He didn't feel feverish, and it was only his head that ached.

"Christ, Max, what did you do?" he asked. Pretty much a rhetorical question since he couldn't remember a thing. Picking up the tiny bottle of cheap motel shampoo, he squeezed a dollop out and began rubbing it into his scalp, doing his best to massage a coherent thought into his head.

A sliver of memory whispered, catching Max's attention. He shut his eyes, trying to focus on it. A dim, unfamiliar interior floated across his internal screen. Light sparking off glassware... maybe bottles, a mirror? A few shadowy figures standing together. Some sitting at tables, two or three... at a bar.

Comprehension dawned, and his eyes popped open.

Right. After he'd checked in to the bed-and-breakfast, he'd left his bags in his room and walked the few blocks to Randy's Rodeo Grill and Bar. The grizzled bartender had offered him a local beer. He'd been thirsty and downed it quickly, then ordered another. An older guy, older than Max anyway, had approached him claiming he knew Max from somewhere. Max had assured the man he'd never been to Collier's Creek before. Radiating disbelief, the man had drifted off, leaving Max on his own again.

After that, things got fuzzy. There was a hint of a man's profile. A conversation. Not the same man who'd thought he knew Max. Shutting his eyes again, allowing the water to continue doing its work, Max stood under the spray for much longer than necessary, coaxing more memories to return.

He'd sat at the bar and quaffed a couple pints of excellent local beer. Had he ordered food? His stomach rumbled painfully. Max didn't think he'd eaten. He was starving this morning. Someone had come in and talked to the bartender for a few minutes. Had they sat down next to Max?

Possibly.

A well-known country singer had been crooning her heart out over the sound system. Max wasn't a huge fan, but he'd been tapping his fingers on the oak bar, figuring he was in Wyoming, after all.

Reaching down to turn off the faucet, Max realized he was humming *Are You Alright,* with Lucinda Williams's voice in his head singing right along with him.

After Lucinda, nothing. Nada.

Heaving a huge sigh, Max dried himself off and dragged yesterday's clothes back on. His wallet was still in the back pocket of his jeans and a quick glance told him his credit cards were all there. He hadn't been robbed. The only thing missing was his jacket, something easily replaceable. And who knew? Maybe he'd left it at the bar.

It was fine. Everything was fine. Nothing happened. Nothing to see here. Just a middle-aged guy having a crisis.

He thanked all that was fucking holy that Delores was busy elsewhere when Max arrived back at the B and B. He was freezing, actually shivering from the chill in the air, and really didn't want to engage with the friendly innkeeper. If he was at all lucky, Delores would never know he'd spent the night somewhere else.

Keeping his head down and ignoring the protest of his muscles, Max darted up the stairs to his room on the third floor. The scent of freshly brewed coffee wafted from the breakfast room, but he didn't want to see or talk to anyone for a few hours. Not until he stopped feeling like four-day-old dead fish.

He'd slunk out of the Wagon Wheel Motel. Lucky him, there'd been no one behind the desk or in the lobby. A twinge of guilt pinged as he'd walked past the desk and dropped the key card in the night slot, but he was just going to assume that the room had been paid for even if he didn't remember doing it. Waking up in the strange bed had been all the mortification he could handle for the moment. For the day, the week, and probably the entire month. Year?

The rest of his life.

If he hadn't paid, he'd figure out some way to make an anonymous donation to the motel. Maybe they could hire someone to fix the culturally inaccurate murals. He'd spotted more of them on his way out. The artist had obviously been given free rein and not been required to fact-check their depictions.

Shutting the door quietly behind him, Max stopped in the center of his room, a lovely corner suite full of light. Light he could do without at the moment. Both windows had a view of the small town and the mountains beyond it, frilly lace curtains framing them on both sides. Across from the view, an oval antique mirror hung on one wall above a massive oak dresser. The floor was a lovely golden hardwood and partially covered by a wool area rug.

An additional benefit? He was the only one there.

Collier's Creek Bed and Breakfast was one of two he'd found listed on the "where to stay in town" site. The Wagon Wheel had not caught his attention. He shuddered. Max had liked that the B and B was supposedly haunted by the spirit of the town's founder, Jack Collier. And, as he'd discovered, it was just a short walk from Randy's Rodeo Grill and Bar.

Maybe he should head back over to the pub later and see if his jacket was there. And if any other memories could be jogged? Maybe it didn't matter. Nothing had happened, after all. He'd even found his cell phone—battery depleted—sitting on the desk back in the other room.

Max's head began to throb painfully again. Heading to his suitcase, he found the bottle of ibuprofen he'd packed, opened it, swallowed three pills, and chugged more water. While waiting for his headache to subside, he moved to the west-facing window and took in the spectacular view of the Tetons.

The stunning mountain range formed the western side of the Jackson Hole region, of which Collier's Creek was a part, but this morning they were hidden, shrouded by thick clouds.

Where Max grew up, clouds usually meant rain, but here he didn't know for certain. It was barely the end of October. Surely there wouldn't be snow this early? There couldn't be; he was driving out to meet his half sister for the first time today. She was the reason he'd traveled from Washington to Wyoming.

"Are you kidding me?" Max muttered. A snowflake at least as big as the Millennium Falcon drifted downward and smacked against his windshield. "It's snowing? For real?"

According to his navigation system, the drive out to Twisted Pine Ranch took approximately forty minutes. Did that take snow into account? Surely this was just a freak storm. The snow would stop in minutes, right? At the very least, it would clear up once he got over this fifteen percent grade hill.

Maybe he should have called and canceled meeting with Robin. It wasn't as if his half sister was suddenly going to sell her ranch and disappear. And he still felt like the walking dead. But Max prided himself on being reliable. If he said he was going to do a thing, he did that thing. He didn't want her to think he was unpredictable. Therefore, no, he wasn't going to turn around and head back to town. The snow was going to stop and he'd be at Twisted Pine soon enough.

These weren't whiteout conditions—at least, Max didn't think so—but the fact that the temperature had dropped and the road narrowed to barely two lanes in both directions had him on edge.

"You're closer to the ranch than town, so just keep going," he told himself as he eyed the navigation system that hadn't reloaded for a few miles. "Slow and steady wins the race."

What a stupid saying.

He risked releasing the steering wheel to jab at the dashboard map. It stubbornly still refused to update where he was. Slow and steady might get you to the finish line, but you wouldn't win the race. Max rolled his eyes at himself. Who cared? This wasn't a race. This was him meeting his half sister for the first time in their lives.

A pair of headlights lit up his rearview mirror, startling him, and Max refocused his attention on the increasingly slippery and winding road. He pressed on the gas, not wanting to irritate the driver behind him. But what he really wanted to do was pull over so they could pass him by.

He tapped against the brakes, intending to pull to the side of the road as much as he could. He did not want to end up several hundred yards down the steep hillside. Cars rarely burst into flame, but Max still had no problem *imagining* that his would be the exception. At that moment, a strong gust of wind buffeted the car and the steering wheel jerked in his grasp.

Max slammed on the brakes even though he knew better.

"Shit!"

Max's life flashed before his eyes as the SUV went into a slow spin, sliding toward the nonexistent shoulder and the no-longer-visible canyon beyond.

His lungs refused to function as the SUV slid a few more feet before finally shuddering to a stop with just inches to spare. Flicking on his hazards, Max sat and stared out at nothing while his heart jackhammered against his ribs.

THREE

Nash

Gritting his teeth, his right hand resting on the stick shift *just in case*, Nash shot a death glare at the quickly disappearing two-lane road in front of him. The southern route into and out of Collier's Creek was fine on a sunny day, but this surprise early snow created havoc for an experienced driver like himself, let alone one from out of state, like the guy leading their two-car caravan up the road.

Where the driver was going Nash couldn't begin to guess— there wasn't much out this way other than privately owned ranch land. And, in five or six hours on a good day, Salt Lake City.

Nash gripped the steering wheel tight enough that his knuckles turned white. If the driver was unsure now, they were going to be a damn mess when the switchbacks they were currently navigating topped the rise of Bear's Claw Canyon and the wind really started to toss them around.

"For fucking fuck's sake."

The red brake lights kept flashing from the back of the late-model SUV fifty yards in front of his own beater pickup truck.

Squinting at it, he didn't recognize the vehicle. Probably some lost tourists wishing they'd listened to the weather forecast.

The snow was coming down fast and hard now. The flakes were huge and, in Nash's imagination, hit the blacktop with an audible thump.

Not for the first time, Nash wished he'd listened to the forecast too, or at least had the truck's radio working again. But crying over spilled milk and all that. Peeling his fingers off the stick shift, he reached over and fiddled with the dials again, but all he got for his effort was static.

The brake lights up ahead flashed again. Nash scowled. The way the fool was driving, their SUV was bound to end up in a ditch. And sooner rather than later.

"For fuck's sake," he growled. His stomach growled in agreement.

Damn, he'd missed lunch and had only had coffee for breakfast. When he finally got to the ranch, Robin was going to take one look at him and shake her head in disgust—before handing him a piece of bread with peanut butter slathered on it.

All his life, he'd forgotten to eat. He could go all day without having anything, but when hunger struck, all bets were off. Robin teased that he was the inspiration for that candy bar commercial where a super grumpy person becomes human again after eating.

He wasn't *that* grumpy, just a little hungry.

As the thought crossed his mind, the SUV braked too hard at nothing that Nash could see and—just as he'd predicted— the car started to spin and slide across the middle line in what seemed like slow motion. The driver panicked and overcorrected, sending the car the other direction. A much more dangerous one because that side had a steep drop-off.

"Fucking fucking hell." There was nothing Nash could do but watch with his heart in his throat and pray to a god he didn't believe in that the car wouldn't go over the edge. Getting a tow up here would be a bitch. Nash wasn't even sure there was cell service at the moment. And who knew if the driver would survive.

The car spun in a slow circle, the headlights momentarily blinding Nash, then, by some fucking miracle, it was back to facing the correct direction *and* still on the road.

"What the actual fuck?" Who got breaks like that?

The person behind the wheel was either an experienced race car driver or lucky as fuck. Nash was going with lucky as fuck.

Flicking on his flashers, Nash pulled to a stop behind the now idling SUV. The heat of the car's exhaust was sending steam billowing upward—which meant the engine was still good, thank god—but the driver's side door didn't open.

It was Nash's duty to check on them. If he thought the idiot with the Washington State plates should be damn thankful they were alive and not in a crumpled heap somewhere toward the bottom of the canyon? Well, he'd keep that to himself.

If they couldn't drive any further today, Nash also had a responsibility to make sure they got somewhere safe—alive and in one piece. It didn't matter where the driver was from or what had put them on the road in front of Nash. No way would a local leave a tourist in this situation without at least checking on them.

Opening his door, he stepped out into the soft, newly fallen snow, glad he'd worn his winter boots. Much like the stranger's car, when Nash breathed out, a vapor cloud formed, momentarily warming his cheeks before dissipating. Sighing again, he tugged his knit cap back over his ears and carefully moved toward the other car, then thumped the side to get the driver's attention, in case for some reason they hadn't seen Nash stop behind them.

He squinted at a colorful decal plastered on one window. The pride rainbow was not something Nash saw a lot of around Collier's Creek. More now than when he'd been growing up, but still rare. And for all he knew, this was just a rainbow and didn't mean anything.

The driver's window stayed rolled up, so Nash tapped a gloved knuckle against it.

"Hello, you okay in there?"

Were they having a medical emergency? He fucking hoped not. A whirring sound began and the window lowered, and Nash was staring at one of the most gorgeous men he'd ever seen in his life.

Again.

It was New Guy, the man he'd escorted to the Wagon Wheel Motel last night. The man who'd invited him to share his bed. Many times. He'd made it difficult for Nash to keep saying no.

Why was the universe fucking with him like this?

Golden-brown eyes blinked back at him and the irises expanded. Nash briefly imagined this was what a galaxy must look like from afar. He sucked a chilly breath of air in through his nose. This was not smart. This was what got men like him in big fucking trouble.

So of course he was an asshole.

"What the fuck was that driving? You're lucky you didn't end up dead. There's no way anybody could get to you down there if you had even survived the fall."

The driver's eyes narrowed, and his lips parted before closing again. They were ragged, as if he'd been biting them while he drove. Nash refused to acknowledge that he was still paying attention to ever-changing amber eyes and arching dark eyebrows. Silver hair streaked with black gleamed in the weird light of the snowstorm and Nash could see that, at most, the man was in his midforties, not even ten years older than he was.

Hello, libido. A lone highway was not the place to be noticing strange men. That was a good way to get beat up or worse. Even if the guy *had* made a very clear overture last night—several over-tures, in fact. Nash recalled the gentle tugs on his belt loops as the man tried to convince him to lie down on the bed with him, the way he'd teased and cajoled Nash until he'd almost given in.

Even if he had a rainbow sticker on one car window, nothing was going to happen.

Probably straight, Nash told himself firmly. An ally, not gay or bi. At the very least, straight when he was sober. Nash had gotten this far in life without getting his ass kicked, he didn't want the streak to end now.

"Hi there, it's lovely to meet you too." The stranger stuck his hand out the open window. "My name's Max."

He didn't remember Nash. That much was crystal clear.

Max. There was something about that name. Nash rolled the word around in his brain as he held Max's gaze for a moment before relenting. He really wanted to continue raging at the guy for being an idiot, but that would have to wait until later.

"Nash. Nash Vigil. How far do you have to go?"

Max released a huge sigh that momentarily fogged his windshield. "I'm not sure. I'm not getting any service now and I accidentally clicked off my navigation app. Now all it's doing is circling the drain."

"Where are you headed?" Nash crowded against the SUV as a truck slowly approached and then stopped next to them, its passenger side window rolling down. Glancing over his shoulder, Nash recognized another Collier's Creek local, Cooper Ellis.

"Coop," he said by way of a greeting.

"Ya'll right, Nash? Need a tow or a call?" Cooper asked, concern lacing his words.

Nash looked back at Max, who didn't answer the question.

"You okay to drive?" he prompted.

Max nodded emphatically. Nash didn't believe him but there wasn't much he could do about that.

"Nah," Nash answered, "but thanks for stopping."

"Be careful," Cooper said seriously. "This damn storm took everybody by surprise. It's not even November yet."

"Over and out. Tomorrow it will be sunny, warm, and a mess."

"Yup." Coop waved, closed the window, and started moving

his truck slowly up the road before disappearing around the next hairpin turn. Nash wondered where he was going but ultimately decided it was none of his business. Nash was all about minding his own business.

"Where are you headed?" Nash asked Max again, doing his best not to sound like he wanted to murder this perfect stranger. He didn't. He wanted to get the man into his bed and ravage him like a pirate. Apparently Nash was way overdue for a hookup.

"Twisted Pine Ranch." Max responded, sending Nash's stomach into a tailspin. *Jesus fucking Christ.* "It's up here somewhere. I think the directions said to turn in a few miles? There'll probably be a sign for it. I'll be fine." The last few words were not at all convincing.

Jesus fucking Christ on a fucking cracker. This guy was *Maximillian Stone.* Nash glanced up at the sky and got a snowflake directly in the eye for his trouble. Of all the people in all the world, Nash had to stop for the one he'd hated forever without ever meeting. Why? Why did this kind of shit happen to him?

Worse, he didn't actually *hate* Stone. He wanted him badly enough it almost physically hurt. Last night had been torture. Not feeling like doing the drive home, he'd crashed at Coop's place and spent the night fantasizing about a slightly older man with amazing eyes and silver in his hair.

"Jesus H. Christ," Nash muttered.

There *was* a signpost for the ranch. There was also an eight-mile stretch of gravel and dirt road between the turnoff and the main house. There was no way Max Stone would get there in one piece and then Nash would have to explain to Robin what had happened.

Oh, I saw the guy but left him on the side of the road back aways. Too bad he didn't make it alive. So sad.

"Is there a problem?" Max asked, bringing Nash back to the current situation. "While I really do appreciate you stopping and ripping me a new asshole"—instead of scared and nervous, Max's voice dripped with sarcasm—"the weather doesn't seem to be getting any better, so I should probably get moving again."

Underneath Nash's glove, the car window started to push upward against his hand. Nash wasn't going to apologize for being hungry and hating that Max Stone was not hateable. But he did have a moral duty to make sure this guy arrived safely at the ranch. Dammit.

"Here's what's gonna happen," Nash said. "I'm going to head back to my truck and then I'm gonna pull up in front of you. *Do not* try and drive away before then. If you do, I'll force you off the road myself and wash my hands of you." Max stared back at him, his eyes narrowed and brows drawn together in what Nash thought was astonishment. Had no one ever given the man a direct order before? "When I'm ahead of you, pull back onto the road and follow me. I'll lead the way to Twisted Pine. Got it?"

Without waiting for an answer, Nash turned and stomped back to his truck. And with each step, he silently berated his stupid dick for wanting something it couldn't have.

FOUR

Max

Max kept one eye on his side mirror and watched the lean stranger—Nash Vigil, who had both the perfect cowboy name and the perfect cowboy ass gorgeously defined by the Wranglers encasing it—stomp back to the beat-up truck parked behind Max's Tahoe. He was tempted to try and drive off, but his heart was still pounding wildly from the near-death experience he'd had only a few minutes ago.

A near-death experience immediately followed by a completely inappropriate attraction. Great. Max knew better. And the attraction was to a stranger who would probably not be ecstatic to learn Max was gay. A man who'd obviously been raised by a family of rabid wolverines.

Max wanted nothing to do with the asshat his guardian angel had thought fit to send, but he guessed he could put up with following his truck until they got to the ranch. The impatient blare of a horn interrupted his thoughts, informing Max that Vigil was ready for him to get with the program already.

Whatever that program was.

Slowly, carefully, Max shifted into Drive and pressed his foot on the gas pedal. The tires slipped once before gripping the slick pavement. Sucking in a deep breath, Max pressed harder on the gas and lurched back onto the road behind Nash Vigil.

Max was a smart man. Something close to loathing had flashed in Vigil's expression when he'd told him his destination was Twisted Pine Ranch. Why? The man either hated Twisted Pine for some reason or Max. Since Max had never met Vigil before, he had to assume it was the ranch. Most people liked Max; it was his twin who rubbed folks the wrong way.

Another long honk alerted Max to the fact that he'd let Vigil get too far ahead of him.

"This guy," he muttered, shaking his head.

Gripping the steering wheel, Max refocused his attention on the battered Ford truck and pushed thoughts of Twisted Pine, and his disgruntled savior, out of his head.

Parking the Tahoe next to Nash Vigil's truck, Max cut the engine and sat for a moment listening to the clicks and creaks as the motor cooled. It had been a bone-rattling fifty-nine minutes—during which the snow began to fall faster and thicker—and Max's anxiety was through the roof. When they turned onto the Twisted Pine driveway at last, they seemed to drive out of the storm, though. The snow had almost stopped and now the late afternoon sun was shining on them.

"Fucking hell."

He was exhausted from focusing on the road and on the truck ahead of him. He'd been petrified that his savior would disappear, leaving him to find his own way. And he'd kept imagining his car careening off the edge of the canyon and not being discovered until spring. He felt lucky he hadn't pissed himself or lost his lunch.

"But I didn't. I made it."

Several other cars, trucks, and ATVs were also parked along-side the three-story barn. It was one of several buildings Max had seen as they'd gotten closer to the main house. With a glittering blanket of snow covering the roofs and the craggy range beyond them, the barns looked like they should be on postcards or in paintings.

The view was stunning. The mountains he'd seen from the bed-and-breakfast appeared to be just miles away, stretching upward toward the now blue sky. Max knew it was an illusion, that the Tetons were still almost one hundred miles from the ranch, but it seemed like a mere ten-minute walk would get him to the foothills.

Popping open his door, Max climbed out of the car and sucked in a lungful of the frigid air as he took in everything he could. He didn't care that he was standing in six inches of snow and his feet were cold. The view was the best tonic for clearing out the last vestige of abject terror he'd felt when the Tahoe had spun out of control on the so-called highway.

Across from where he stood was the main house, a long, low-slung, one-story affair protected from the wind by a stand of—no surprise—pine trees. A covered porch looked like it wrapped around most of the house and on it were several wooden chairs, strategically placed so viewers could sit and watch the world go by. Or the sun set. Maybe the sunrise? Max had no sense of direction.

Without saying anything, Vigil stomped off toward the house, leaving Max to follow. Or maybe not. Maybe he wished Max would fall into a snow bank and disappear. Shrugging, Max trailed after him. As they drew closer, the front door opened and a woman stepped out, waving at them.

He and Robin had exchanged photos via email so Max imme-diately recognized his half sister. And of course she'd known he was coming. He'd spent ages comparing himself and his identical twin to the photos he'd received. Max and Xavier took after their mom for the most part, but he'd noticed that all three of them shared the same shape of nose and jawline. And, like Max and Xavier, Robin's hair was more salt than pepper.

"Nash, I wasn't sure you'd make it back from town," she exclaimed, a smile creasing her cheeks. "Who'd you bring with you?" Peering closer at Max, recognition dawned on her face. "Max? Max Stone? It's you!"

"In the flesh." Max returned Robin's smile with enthusiasm. He couldn't help himself; her grin was infectious.

Robin had known he was traveling to Wyoming to meet her, of course. Max would never show up unannounced at a newly discovered relative's house. But he hadn't been sure how long the drive from Washington would take, and what with the nasty weather surprise and him nearly dying in it, he hadn't texted her that he was close. Originally, he'd just thought he would stop by and get the awkward-greeting part over before returning to Collier's Creek, but now he didn't know if he'd be able to make the drive back today.

"Get yourself up here so we can meet for real! I can't believe you're here."

Max couldn't believe it either.

A year ago, Max had discovered a terrible truth about his biological father and that truth had led him to reach out to Robin Simpson, the owner of Twisted Pine Ranch. Robin was the older half sister of Max and his twin, Xavier. To be fair, it wasn't the first Terrible Truth about his shitbag of a father, but it was a doozy.

It was lovely to discover you were the second family of a cheater. Bad enough his sack-of-shit father hadn't cared enough about his twin sons or their mom to stick around, but Craig Stone had already been married with a baby daughter when he'd arrived in Cooper Springs and swept Wanda off her feet.

Max and Robin had been emailing back and forth for a while now—against his brother's advice. Just another way he and Xavier were different. A while back, Max had decided he wanted to meet his older sister in person. He wished he could erase the swath of damage his jackass of a father had left behind him.

He couldn't change the past, but Max hoped he could change the future, and extending an olive branch could go a long way. The ranch was in trouble, a simple internet search had shown him that. And since Max had plenty of money, more than he knew what to do with, he hoped he could help Robin out without a big deal being made about it.

But was he even doing the right thing? He paused midstep.

Maybe it was from nearly driving off a cliff, but Max was suddenly second-guessing every decision he'd made that led him to this point. What if Robin hated him? What if he hated her? What if his brother was right that there was no righting the kind of wrong their father had done and that it wasn't Max's responsibility to try anyway? He bit his lip. A few feet from him, Vigil released an impatient sigh and stormed up the porch steps into the house without so much as a by-your-leave.

"Don't mind him," Robin said in the vacuum he'd left behind. "He probably forgot to eat. Nash is notoriously hangry."

"I am not," Vigil denied from somewhere inside.

"He totally is and won't admit it until he's had food."

Max paused in front of Robin, not sure what to do now. He'd come all this way and nearly died in the process. Did they hug? Shake hands? Wave?

Still smiling, Robin solved the problem by stepping close and quickly wrapping her arms around him.

"Come on in," she said after releasing him again and nodding her head toward the door, "and I'll see if I can't make a human out of Nash."

. . .

The front room had a plain but comfortable interior, although someone who lived there like to play a variety of musical instruments. A few guitars hung against the walls and an upright piano with sheet music propped against the keys sat across from a sectional. Max wondered if Robin played or if it was someone else. A massive stone fireplace took up one wall with another sectional-style couch arranged in front of it.

What Max really wanted to get a better look at was the bookshelf jammed into the remaining space. As they walked past it, he spotted Robin Cook thrillers, Tom Patterson novels, and old Zane Grey paperbacks. Bookshelves were a glimpse into a reader's soul, and with a house as old as this one, he could learn a lot just by skimming the titles.

He wanted to stop and peruse the books, but instead Robin led Max into the dining room. He made a note to investigate the shelves another time.

"We all eat here in the winter. As you can see, Twisted Pine used to be busier. We had a lot of visitors and employees back in the day."

Like the living room, the dining area was simply decorated. A few framed black-and-white pictures hung above a sideboard and in the middle of the floor was a table large enough to fit at least twelve people.

"And here is the true center of our universe," Robin announced, gesturing at another door like a Wheel of Fortune host. "The kitchen. Come on in."

Max followed Robin into the large room. Well-used pots and pans dangled from a stainless-steel rack hanging from the ceiling and over a wide kitchen island. Several chairs were placed around the island, and he could easily imagine sitting there with coffee while people planned out their days. In one corner, he spotted a desktop computer set up in what might have once been a pantry, but the door had been removed and a tabletop was mounted to the wall with a chair tucked under it. A calendar was tacked above the makeshift desk and several manila file folders were stacked on it.

Vigil had the refrigerator door open but appeared to be frozen there, staring at the contents as if something was going to randomly fling itself out and into his mouth. If Max's mom had been there, she would've made a snarky comment about not using the fridge to cool the house.

"Watch this," Robin muttered under her breath. Max crossed his arms over his chest and leaned against the island. Opening a cabinet to her right, Robin pulled down a sleeve of bagels and a massive jar of Adam's peanut butter and set them on the counter. She quickly cut the bagel apart and slathered it with thick swathes of the peanut butter but didn't bother to set it on a plate.

"Yo, Nash Vigil, if you can hear me, turn around."

Nash didn't immediately respond. Robin rolled her eyes, making Max snicker—very quietly. The last thing he needed was to piss this guy off and, even though he'd been a good Samaritan on the road, he obviously didn't like Max.

Max was still a bit shocked that he'd nearly run off the road and the driver behind him had been heading to Twisted Pine as well, even more so than he'd been by the near-death experience itself. How weird was that? And now the same stranger was being force-fed bagels by his recently discovered half sister.

Did things like this happen a lot in Collier's Creek, or was Max just the lucky one?

Shutting the fridge, Nash finally turned around and scowled in Max and Robin's direction, which seemed about par for the course. Max decided not to take it personally.

Robin held the bagel out toward Nash as if she was enticing a wild animal to come and eat from her hand. Nash's dark gaze landed on the offering. Snatching it from her, he took a huge bite and began chewing, his cheeks bulging like a squirrel's.

"Nash has a hanger management issue."

Nash mumbled something unintelligible.

Robin rolled her eyes again. "I swear this man needs a keeper. He forgets to eat and then acts like it's normal to morph into a honey badger protecting its territory."

The younger man scowled harder and Max worked hard to repress his smile. He had the distinct feeling that, hangry or not, Nash Vigil didn't like him. That was fine. Not going to take it personally, he reminded himself.

"Would you like something to drink?" Robin asked Max. "Coffee, tea?"

"Coffee? I shouldn't stay long. I don't know how long it will take to drive back to the B and B." Even as he uttered the words, he knew he couldn't drive back to town, but he needed to at least make the effort.

Nash coughed and rasped, his face turning red. For a second, Max thought he was angry again, but Robin rushed around the island to bang him on the back.

"What have I told you about breathing and eating?" she joked. "Breathe then swallow, never both at the same time."

Managing to scowl harder, Nash chewed and swallowed the last of his bagel. "There's no way you're making it back into Collier's Creek today," he informed Max. Turning to Robin, he said, "He already almost ended up in the canyon. Doesn't even have snow tires on his car."

"It's still fall!" Max protested.

"And looky there." Nash pointed out the kitchen window. "It snowed."

If Nash was trying to make Max feel stupid, it was working.

"Nashville Todd Vigil," Robin said with a scowl of her own, "mind your manners. I don't know what crawled up your butt and died there, but knock off the attitude." To Max she said, "Nash does have a good point though. I'll make up a bed for you in one of the spare rooms. That way I won't have to worry about you ending up in the canyon."

"No, really. That's too much," he protested weakly. "I just

wasn't prepared and the snow was falling so fast." He looked out the window. "It seems to have stopped."

Robin looked too. "It has stopped, and tomorrow it will melt away. But just to stay on the safe side and out of the emergency room, you'll stay here," she said in a tone that brooked no argument—he'd never tell her but it reminded him of his mom. "Give Delores a call and let her know the plan. She won't mind."

With a final glare at Max plus a roll of his eyes *and* shake of his head, Vigil left the kitchen, departing through a door opposite the one they'd come in through.

Max watched him, wondering what he'd done to make the man hate him. Clearly, he wasn't on board with Max staying at the ranch. Or on board with Max at all.

"Don't worry about him. Nash is protective and likes to think he knows what's best. Please, stay."

"Okay," Max agreed. "Just for tonight though. Tomorrow I'll head back to the bed-and-breakfast."

Robin rubbed her hands together gleefully. "Excellent. I'll get your room ready. Are you vegetarian? I know it's cliché, but it's chili night on the ranch. If that doesn't work for you, I could make you a sandwich or something."

"Nope, not vegetarian. Chili sounds great."

"Great. You go grab your stuff. If you need any clothes, Nash or Burl can loan you something. You'll be the second door down the hallway off the living room, so meet me there. Supposedly, Teddy Roosevelt slept in that room when he traveled through the area in 1883. I doubt it's true, but you never know."

Robin dashed off. At least she seemed happy to see him. What was Vigil to Robin anyway? And did he matter? Max shook his head. This was Robin's home, she wanted him there, so he would stay for the night. Nash Vigil would just have to live with it. But no way in hell was he borrowing anything from him.

FIVE

Nash

Nash shut his bedroom door and threw his rucksack on his bed. Hands on his hips, he stared out the window toward the craggy hills that surrounded Twisted Pine Ranch.

What was Stone's angle? The man wanted something. Nash did not trust long-lost relatives in any shape or form. Max was not Nash's relative, not by blood anyway—Robin was Nash's cousin by marriage—but he still didn't trust Stone. The marriage bringing Robin and Nash together had failed many years ago, but Nash had stayed on at Twisted Pine because he loved both it and his ex-step-cousin.

Nash loved Robin (*as a sister*, he did not swing that way) but she was not the best business person. Robin was a people person. All people and animals gravitated to her—like Snow White, all the creatures in the forest and on the ranch loved her. And Robin, trustingly, loved them all back. How many times over the years had she taken in folks down on their luck? Most had been honest people but one or two had needed Nash and Burl to help them move along. Her lack of judgment sometimes made Nash want to pull his hair out. If he'd kept it longer, he might actually have been tugging on it right now.

Rolling his neck, he left his room and walked back down the hallway, his stomach no longer rumbling. He ignored the voices coming from the kitchen and pushed through the outer door to step out onto the porch. The temperature had dropped even further and he wasn't wearing a heavy coat, but he still flopped down in one of the handmade log chairs with a disgruntled thump. At least the bagel Robin had given him had taken the edge off his hunger.

The clouds were already starting to disappear, and Nash figured the snow would be melted by lunch tomorrow, maybe earlier. Now that he'd conveniently been stranded at Twisted Pine, would Max Stone leave then? Damn, he hoped so. The last thing Robin needed was another predatory asshole getting his claws into the ranch.

Twisted Pine was nearly two thousand acres of gorgeous, pristine forest and pasture-slash-grazing land. Over a decade ago, Robin made the decision to focus on tourism as the best way to keep the ranch afloat. It was perfect for folks wanting the cowboy experience, plus they still had cattle and now goats. Nash thought it was hilarious that people wanted to pay to muck stalls and drive cattle, but whatever floated their boat.

She'd put Nash in charge of most of the accounting side of Twisted Pine—a good choice since he was *not* a people person. But even with everything they'd done, they were still having a hard time paying the bills on time.

And now there was an interloper. Crossing his arms over his chest, he tucked his hands under them to keep warm. He needed more time to think before dinner. And, hopefully, to get his temper under control.

As soon as Robin had told Nash about her "new half brother," he'd hunted down whatever he could find on Max Stone, proving that the internet was good for something other than rando hookups.

After first falling down a rabbit hole involving Marvel, Earthmover, and Ultimo, Nash easily found the real-life Maximillian Stone.

Stone was almost as interesting as Earthmover and probably as smart. His LinkedIn bio was all Nash had needed. The guy had graduated from MIT and been recruited by several software companies before eventually going to some big name in Silicon Valley. The short story was that Stone was a millionaire several times over. He'd left the software industry behind and was now "searching for the next thing."

Gross, how new-agey was that? Maybe he wanted to raise llamas or grow hemp. Or worse, mine for precious metals. Were there deposits on Twisted Pine property? More than likely. Were they rich enough to justify ruining the land? No.

But why else would a millionaire reach out to Robin? Why else would he visit if not to scope it out and find out just how much financial trouble they were in and how cheaply he could buy the land Nash loved with all his heart?

"Fucker."

He heard the front door open and then close again with a bang. A few seconds later, the sound of a car door opening reached Nash's ears. Stone was getting his stuff out of his car. Wasn't that just dandy?

From late spring to early fall, all staff and guests on the ranch ate their meals together in the largest refurbished barn. Paying guests felt like they were getting the full cowboy experience and it was good for the staff to meet them too. This time of year, when the staff was reduced to Robin, Nash, and a few permanent hands, they all ate together at the big house.

There was also Burl Montgomery, who'd been the stock manager for decades but had retired a few years ago and now was the acting hash-slinger. Guests loved the big, gruff cowboy. In reality, he was a total pushover who during high season could often be found hanging out with the younger guests and telling ghost stories of the old days. So much for retiring.

Nash and Burl had their own bedrooms in the main house and Robin had gifted each of them small parcels of their own. Nash hadn't wanted to accept, but Robin had raised the biggest stink on the planet, the gist of which was, "I can't pay you enough, self-sacrificing, blah blah." Then she'd said he could use one of the barns for his goats if he said yes, so he'd caved.

The rest of the guys were spread out between two bunkhouses that had basic kitchens with the means to make the most important meal of the day: coffee.   Even so, Robin liked everyone around the table for dinner. She claimed laying eyes on them every day was important. Personally, Nash could go days without seeing anyone, but whatever floated her boat.

On the plus side, Burl could cook and Nash couldn't make anything more than Top Ramen.

Nash nodded his chin at the McDonald brothers, Kellen and Harley, as he took his normal spot at the oversized pine dining table. Normally he helped set out the plates, but tonight he'd stayed outside until Burl rang the bell. Now he felt slightly guilty —he wasn't the kind of person to avoid chores.

He just hated Max Stone. Whom he could hear talking to Robin in the kitchen.

"Where's Radko?" Nash asked, noting there were seven settings.

"Got stuck in town," Kellen said with a grin. "I think it was accidentally on purpose."

"We think he likes somebody but he won't tell us who."

"I wonder why not?" Nash said sarcastically. "Maybe because you two like to spread news wider than TMZ."

The brothers glanced at each other and then tried puppy-dog eyes on Nash. "We do not!" they protested in tandem.

"You know," Nash said, not for the first time, "it's a good thing there're two of you because of the shared-brain thing."

"My mom said my twin and I shared a brain," Max said as he stepped into the dining room. In his hands was a pan Nash knew held fresh-baked cornbread. "At least until we started school, then things changed." Carefully, he set the pan down on a cork pad in the middle of the table.

"We've got the rest, Max. Just make yourself comfortable," Robin called out.

The seat next to Nash hadn't been claimed and usually Radko sat next to Harley. Max eyed Nash and chose Radko's seat. For some reason, that pissed Nash off. Snagging the edge of the hot pan, he pulled it toward his plate and dug out his favorite, a corner piece of cornbread.

"Dude, you always do that. There's only four corner pieces!" Harley looked outraged. Probably because he knew Kellen would take one and he had to offer their guest the third one. They all knew to leave a corner for Burl.

"You snooze, you lose," Nash said heartlessly.

"There better be a corner piece when I get in there!" Burl called from the kitchen.

Nash smirked and handed the spatula to Kellen.

Burl came into the room carrying a vat of chili and Robin followed him with the salad she insisted was part of a well-balanced meal. She wasn't wrong, Nash just hated salad. No doubt Max Stone would love the slimy, nasty greens.

Clearly, everyone had already been introduced to Max so Nash didn't have to suffer through a round of "getting to know you." While the rest of them served themselves and chatted, he spooned chili into his mouth and listened to the conversation flowing around him.

"So, Max, your first time visiting our fair state?" Burl asked.

Max nodded. "It is. I never traveled much as a kid and," he added, smiling, "Wyoming is beautiful but not a software hub."

"But you're retired now, right?" Burl said around a bite.

Nash wasn't the only one who'd done some snooping about Max Stone.

"Yep. Sold my company a couple years ago and the rest is history, as they say."

"Lucky you," Harley interjected. "I'd love to be retired."

"You hardly work as it is." Nash couldn't help himself. "You're pre-retired."

"Hey, I work! I do my part," Harley protested, scowling at Nash.

"Retirement has its benefits," Max said. "But it's not as if I just sit around all day. I like to keep busy."

Busy planning takeovers of ranches, probably. Nash glared across the table at their guest.

"Did you win the lottery?" Kellen wanted to know.

"Nah." Max tapped his forehead. "Brains and a little luck. I was a software developer, had my own company for a while. Got lucky with timing too, but when I wasn't enjoying it anymore, I got out." He frowned. "Probably waited a bit too long to leave the software world though. It's cutthroat." He shrugged as if being a CEO in Silicon Valley was nothing.

Nash shoved a huge bite of cornbread in his mouth to keep from asking his own question. While he had no intention of welcoming this stranger into his—Robin's—home, he was curious about him. What did he mean by waiting too long?

"Where do you call home?" Burl asked.

"Good question. Cooper Springs, I guess. It's on the Washington State coast. A flyspeck really. But I haven't lived there for a long time."

"Ooooh," Kellen said breathlessly. "The land of the Sasquatch. Have you ever seen him?"

Nash snorted and rolled his eyes, accidentally catching Max's glance of amusement. *Of course* Kellen would ask that question, and he was serious too. The kid was obsessed with anything completely unbelievable. Aliens? Yes. Sasquatch? Yeti? El Chupacabra? Trolls? All yes.

"I personally have never seen a Sasquatch, but there are plenty in town who claim they have. My mom's boyfriend—is that the right word for the over-sixty crowd?" He shook his head. "Anyway, Rufus is president of the Bigfoot Society in town."

"Whoa, that is awesome." Kellen's eyes were the size of saucers.

Harley elbowed his brother in the ribs. "Don't get him started," he said to Max. "He'll never stop."

"Just like Mick Jagger," Burl said.

Everyone at the table turned to stare at the craggy ex-stock manager.

"It's a song by the Rolling Stones. *Start Me Up*. You reprobates have heard of the Rolling Stones, right?"

Kellen squinted at him. "That's almost modern-day, Burl. Next thing, you'll be listening to Britney."

Burl shut one eye as if he was thinking hard. "I don't know a Britney."

Kellen's mouth dropped open while a look of disbelief crossed Harley's face, and Robin was clearly hiding a smile. Nash refused to look at Max. He knew full well that Burl was pulling Kellen's leg.

Just another dinner at the Twisted Pine, but this time there was an interloper.

After dinner and dishes, Nash went to his room instead of joining everyone in the living room. Robin gave him a look and rolled her eyes when he gave the excuse of being tired. She probably thought he was sulking.

Was he sulking? No. He shook off the thought as he shut his bedroom door behind him. He really was tired and tomorrow he'd be up early like he always was.

Grabbing his Kindle, he flopped onto the bed and let himself be distracted by rogue vampires who fell in love with humans and together they saved the world. No horses, cattle, or goats involved.

And no Maximillian Stone.

He was naked. The other man was naked. Nash didn't clearly remember what they'd been doing or why they were wherever they were now. Something involving blood pacts, the palest of skin, and ultimate submission. It didn't matter. What did matter was the man in the bed. They'd waited so long to be together. Eons, it felt like. The instant he'd seen him, he'd known the stranger was his. His to claim.

"Come closer," the stranger said, beckoning Nash with languid fingers. "Lie with me."

Kneeling, Nash allowed his body to slowly relax into the mattress. They were close enough that he felt the heat of their bodies mingle and flow between them. He could almost smell it, wanted to touch it.

The blaze was an inferno, but Nash didn't care if he got burned. He was so fucking hot and so fucking hard for this man. Nash wanted the stranger in a way he hadn't wanted anyone in years. He knew it was wrong but their tale was a long one, their world at last saved. They deserved something for their labor.

With the abruptness that only occurs in a dream, the stranger was covering Nash with his body. Their erections fleetingly brushed together. Nash's hips surged upward, wanting more pressure.

Needing more of the touch, he reached out and tried to pull the stranger closer, but it was like trying to grasp smoke. He wanted to see him, to know him. Peering into the dark, he saw the man turn his head. With a shock that almost startled him out of his dream, Nash recognized Maximillian Stone.

Dream Max was just as sexy as the real one.

"What are you doing here?" he wanted to know.

Dream Max didn't answer him and Nash decided he didn't care. Reaching between their bodies, Nash wrapped his fingers around his erection.

"Mmm," he groaned, pumping into his hand.

Nash's eyes popped open. He blinked as the walls of his room came into focus.

There was no dream man, no dream Max. Nash shut his eyes again.

It was just pathetic Nash, alone in bed with his hand wrapped around his cock like a fourteen-year-old boy. He wasn't sure which pissed him off more, that Max Stone had invaded his dream or that he had a throbbing hard-on and no immediate satisfaction for it.

"Fuck me."

SIX

Max

Dinner was fun and Max learned a lot about the Twisted Pine crew. Although, as soon as he finished eating, Nash muttered something about being tired and needing to take a shower before he went to bed. Watching him depart, Max still couldn't shake the eerie feeling that he seemed familiar. It was like looking at smoke and wanting the shape of it to stay the same. He'd never met the man before, he told himself again.

Right?

After clearing up, everyone—except Nash—headed into the living room. Max trailed behind, still mentally poking at the odd feeling in the center of his chest. He forced himself to push his weird feelings aside because they didn't matter. Burl got a fire going in the fireplace and once it was crackling and popping, they all claimed their places on the comfy if well-worn couches and began talking about nothing and everything.

Max learned Kellen and Harley had worked for Twisted Pine for almost five years and almost three years, respectively, both signing on after they'd graduated from high school. They'd grown up outside Cheyenne. Burl had been there for fifty, which meant he'd been around when Craig Stone had been juggling two families. He was nice enough not to bring it up. Probably everyone in the room knew the very sordid Stone family history, but Max still appreciated not being raked over the coals for something that had been entirely out of his control.

He had the financial wherewithal to make things better for Twisted Pine—much better. Hopefully, with luck and persuasion, Robin would see reason and let Max take care of a few outstanding loans.

With little to add to the conversation, Max let himself fade into the background and listen to the chatter. It was clear they all cared for each other—even the brothers, who were much younger than everyone else. The talk swirled around him, full of laughter and teasing. These people were a family.

Around ten or so, Burl cracked a massive yawn. "Time for me to hit the sack."

"It's time we all went to bed." Robin announced, putting a stop to the fireside chat. "Kellan and Harley, don't forget you have a long day tomorrow."

The brothers were heading out to check something somewhere on ranch property. Cows, horses, Max wasn't sure. What he knew about daily ranch life wouldn't fill a post-it note.

Kellen groaned. "Why do we have to do it?"

"Because it's your turn," Burl said as he stood up and moved to the fireplace, grabbing a poker so he could pull the logs apart. Sparks shot up the chimney as the wood shifted and settled again.

"Life on a ranch is definitely not what you see at the movies," Robin said.

"What?" Max widened his eyes. "No bad guys lurking in a canyon trying to steal gold from a lost treasure mine?"

"We wish there was a lost treasure," Burl grumbled as he exited the room.

Minutes later, Max was lying in bed, covered up to the chin

with a thick blanket and colorful comforter. He expected to fall asleep quickly after the day he'd had. Instead, his brain wandered back to the enigma that was Nash Vigil.

When he finally drifted off, he fell into a dream involving a smiling, laughing cowboy and his herd of tripping goats.

Max woke with a start, The jarring sound of a door slamming shut somewhere in the house forcing him awake. He had no way to prove it, but his gut told him the slam had been purposeful and that the perpetrator was one Nash Vigil. Fine. He was awake now, he might as well get out of bed.

The first thing he noticed after dragging himself off the extremely comfortable mattress he'd spent the night on was that snow had melted away just like everyone had said it would. Grumbling, Max pulled on yesterday's jeans and the thick wool sweater his mom had knitted for him. A few minutes later, he shambled into the kitchen where he found Robin sitting at her kitchen office desk and staring at the computer monitor.

"There's a mug on the counter for you," Robin said from where she was working on the computer. "Milk and creamer are in the fridge."

"Thanks." Max stepped over to pick up the cup.

"Your drive back into Collier's Creek should be less eventful than your drive out. Just take it easy. You never know if there's black ice."

"Will do." He had the urge to ask Robin questions about Nash Vigil. He'd immediately thought of him this morning, even before his eyes popped open. "That was some storm," he said, pausing to look out at the snow-free driveway. If he hadn't experienced it yesterday, Max never would have believed it had happened.

"The next snowfall will be the one that sticks around, and it might not melt until April or even May."

Max shuddered and took another sip of coffee. He wasn't sure if he liked the thought of six months of the white stuff or not.

With the steaming mug of coffee in his possession, Max left Robin to her tasks. He'd wanted to offer his help but was certain she would refuse. He was a relative stranger, after all. He snorted —and a strange relative.

The living room still smelled slightly smoky from the fire the night before, and out the front window he immediately spotted Nash doing something cowboy-ish over by the barn. Of course.

When the man wasn't sneering at Max, he was startlingly attractive. Max couldn't pin it down to one thing about him. Yes, he had pretty eyes and a nice smile, not that it had been aimed at Max. There was something else though, something more, something that felt oddly familiar.

Even last night at dinner, when he'd been shooting eye-daggers at Max across the dining room table, Max had felt himself drawn to him. His attention kept shifting to the younger man, like it was now. He'd laughed with Robin and Burl while Nash teased the two brothers about Bigfoot and generally gave them a hard time. The brothers were ridiculous. They reminded Max a little of Xavier and himself *before* Max had left for college. Before Xavier had been betrayed and ambushed by a so-called date.

A dark feeling blossomed in his chest, filling him with tingling anxiety. That would explain a lot about Nash's reaction to Max. He hated to presume that Robin had told her manager that Max was gay and the man was a massive homophobe. But... he was going to go ahead and assume until he knew better. Maybe the guy had seen the rainbow flag sticker on the back of his car? Who knew? But it was better to assume and be safe than just go along and be sorry.

No more ogling fine cowboy ass.

· · ·

Several hours later, Max pulled the Tahoe to the curb in front of the Collier's Creek Bed and breakfast. *Again.* Cutting the engine, he just sat for a second, taking in the cute 1890s-style building he'd be staying in for the next few weeks. Realizing he was holding his breath, he exhaled again, trying to rid himself of feelings he hadn't predicted.

The new pinchy sensation in the center of his chest? That was a sense of disappointment. The B and B was cute. It was all Western and cowboy. But it wasn't the well-worn ranch house and the quirky cast of characters that made up Twisted Pine.

Robin had offered him a room but, aside from Nash Vigil hating his guts, Max felt staying there wasn't the right thing to do. At least, that's what he was telling himself. He wanted to get to know Robin, yes, but taking up residence at the ranch seemed like an imposition. By staying in town, he could become friends with her without invading her space. He'd invite her for a dinner at one of the nicer restaurants in town so they could spend time together, things like that.

But could some place in Collier's Creek really be considered neutral ground? It wasn't, was it? Robin had grown up on the ranch, but the town was her territory as well.

When he'd decided on this trip, Max hadn't taken the size of the town into consideration. At just around nine thousand residents, it was a bit bigger than Cooper Springs, but he doubted the gossip mill would be any less effective, especially once people figured out who he was. At least staying in town meant that Max wouldn't feel the heat of Nash's oddly familiar glare 24-7.

SEVEN

Max

The flutter of the lacy white curtain hanging across one of the front windows of the B and B caught Max's attention. Delores was probably wondering what he was doing sitting in his car instead of coming inside.

Why was he hesitating?

The memory of a set of stormy blue eyes and a fierce scowl gave him pause, and his stomach abruptly twisted. Maybe he shouldn't have come to Collier's Creek? Maybe he should've just let sleeping dogs lie and all that. Maybe Xavier had been right all along—and boy did he not want to deal with his brother acting like a know-it-all on top of everything else.

The B and B's ornate front door opened and then Delores was waving at Max, gesturing for him to come inside. With a rueful smile at his own indecision, Max popped open his car door.

. . .

"Just let me know if you need anything! I can get some sandwich things out if you need them," Delores reminded him as she pulled the bedroom door closed, taking her whirlwind of energy with her.

"What is wrong with me?" Max muttered under his breath. "Nothing, that's what." But even as he spoke, a visual of the mountains that surrounded Twisted Pine rose in his mind. Was it possible to fall in love at first sight with a landscape?

What he needed to do was explore Collier's Creek and get a better lay of the land. What made this small town tick? Max was nothing if not naturally curious.

He wanted to check out the locally owned bookstore and then grab an early dinner at one of the pubs. Robin had tried to get him to agree to dinner at the ranch, but Max figured he'd let Robin and the rest of the Twisted Pine folks get used to the idea of him before he imposed on them again. He'd wanted to say yes though.

Something told him Nash Vigil never planned on getting used to him. Why that left a bad taste in his mouth, Max couldn't put a finger on. He didn't care if Vigil liked him or not, he reminded himself. Nash Vigil was not the reason he was in Collier's Creek.

Max's phone chimed, dragging him out of his Nash Vigil centric thoughts. Tugging it out of his pocket, he glanced at the screen.

Xav scrolled across the top.

He'd meant to call his brother, but with one thing—nearly running off the road—and another—the enigmatic Nash Virgil— he hadn't gotten around to it. If he didn't answer, though, his brother would just keep calling. He might as well get it over with.

"Xav," he said after pressing Accept.

"Bro, you don't call, you don't write! Mom was worried something happened. Did you get there okay?"

"Yeah, I made it. Just a sec." With his phone in one hand, Max checked to be sure he had his room key—*an honest-to-god real key*—

and stepped out onto the landing, locking his door behind him. Delores was nowhere in sight and he didn't hear her talking, so he took the opportunity to jog back down the staircase and out through the front door. "Sorry about that. I'm headed out to grab some grub."

The snow-filled clouds had disappeared and the sun was shining extra brightly, making Max squint and wish he'd grabbed his sunglasses. It was cold enough out that he regretted misplacing his jacket. His stomach chipped in, voicing its displeasure at being ignored.

"So, what's going on?" Xavier asked.

Now Max frowned. "What do you mean, what's going on?"

There was a loud silence on the other end of the line. Damn. Of the two of them, Max was the one who called his brother out, not the other way around.

"Something's going on," Xavier stated, breaking the silence.

There wasn't anything going on. Not really. He may have sort of fantasized about Nash Vigil, but nothing had happened. And Nash had made it clear that nothing ever would. Maybe it was the near-death experience he'd had?

The damn twin connection. For most of their forty-plus years, Max had been the one who'd instinctively known when Xavier needed him. When they were eighteen, he'd already been away at college when a massive bout of dread had him on high alert. After several panicked phone calls home, he'd learned his brother had been attacked by a date. That had been the most intense time, but there were plenty of other examples. And now the shoe was on the other foot and Max wasn't sure he liked it.

"I don't know what you're talking about," he deflected, knowing it was useless.

"Uh-huh," Xavier scoffed. "Try again."

Heading down the sidewalk in the general direction of the pub, Max confessed to his twin about how he'd accidentally gotten drunk and ended up in a strange hotel room.

"And then, as luck would have it, when I decided to drive out to meet Robin yesterday, there was a freak snowstorm. I nearly slid off the road."

"Jesus, Max."

"Yeah," Max agreed. "It's been a day or twenty. The driver behind me made sure I got to the ranch, even if he was the world's biggest asshole. I'm not really sure what I did, but Nash Vigil does not like me."

Although Max hadn't missed the sideway glances that Nash slid his way when he thought Max wasn't paying attention. Maybe he was devising ways to get Max to leave and never come back. Or dispose of the body. Max shook off the thought—that was definitely Xavier's influence.

"Who is this guy?" Xavier wanted to know.

Looking both ways, Max stepped off the curb. Down the block a bit, a blue pickup slowed and let him cross the street. The driver lifted their fingers from the steering wheel and Max nodded back, not able to see their face clearly. Some things about small towns were the same no matter what state they were located in.

Max blew out a gust of air as he answered, "He's the ranch manager for Twisted Pine. At least for most of the financials, it sounds like."

"What's not to like about you, Max? You're polite, smart, and you shower on a regular basis."

Max smiled. His brother was doing his best to make him feel better.

"Right? I'm stellar in the personal cleanliness department. I have no idea what it is. But it doesn't matter. Robin seems to be fine with me, and the rest of the staff didn't seem to have a problem either."

He went on to tell Xavier about dinner the night before.

"Cowboys, Max," Xav gasped. "You are talking about real cowboys. Do they wear chaps?"

Max couldn't help but smile more. Xavier liked cowboys too.

"Real cowboys, but I haven't seen any chaps yet. Maybe your sexy neighbor will wear some for Halloween?"

"Pfft, Barone is too uptight for something like that."

"Don't even try and tell me you aren't imagining him in chaps right now."

There was a pause before Xavier replied, "Fuck off."

Max knew with absolute certainty that Xavier had been visualizing Vincent Barone in tight leather pants and possibly a vest—but nothing else.

"Enough about Barone, fill me in on everything."

By the time Max had run out of words, he'd arrived at the front entrance to Randy's. He was hungry and thirsty, and his brother sometimes wore him out.

"I'll talk to you later, 'k?"

"Sure thing, bro. Don't be a stranger or I'll sic Mom on you."

EIGHT

Nash

"Nashville Todd Vigil." Robin pinned Nash with a heated glare. "What the hell is going on with you? Why were you such an ass to Max last night?"

Crap, full-named by Robin twice in less than two days. Nash sucked in a breath. It was well after lunch time, and he'd slunk back into the kitchen, hoping to grab coffee and something to eat without running into Robin. He should have known better.

He'd spent the last several hours taking care of half-finished chores and making some fence repairs in the south paddock that Kellen or Harley should have already taken care of. He was going to have to have a conversation with the brothers about getting the job done.

He'd fed the goats—*the trip*—and snickered as he did so, recalling Max's pure wonder over the term. Then it had been Ricardo's turn, the chestnut-colored horse he normally rode, followed by Buttercup, a placid beast who was often assigned to newer or hesitant riders.

After that, he'd inspected a leaking sprinkler line and chopped more firewood to add to the woodpile. Nash knew Max was gone because he'd been watching from inside the barn when the man climbed into his SUV and headed back toward town.

He'd thought he was safe. Damn.

Cup of coffee in hand, he turned to face his inquisitor. Robin stood up from her desk, reading glasses perched on the end of her nose. She was as tall as he was and absolutely did not intimidate him the same way she had when he'd been sixteen. And he wasn't gripping his cup handle just a bit tighter.

"I don't trust him," Nash stated baldly. His stomach twisted at his words telling the lie. In reality, Max Stone was too easy to trust. Especially when he was slightly drunk and humming a Britney Spears medley under his breath.

Robin shook her head. "We've been over this before, Nash. I trust Max. He's done nothing that makes me want to change my mind. There are no warning flags. In fact, now that I've met him in person, I like him even more."

"You trust too easily."

This was an argument they'd had before and not just about Max Stone. Robin *did* trust too easily. That loan she'd taken out was a prime example. Robin, on the other hand, claimed he disliked people on first sight.

And what was wrong with that? At least he wasn't constantly disappointed when people behaved badly—as they often did.

"You're not changing my mind," she said. There was a mulish tint to Robin's voice that told Nash he was treading on thin ice. "We've been in each other's pockets a long time, but this time I'm the one who's right. Max doesn't need to prove he's a worthy person. I already know he is in my heart. Just like I've always known you're a good person, even when you were ten and giving me the stink eye." The last part she said with a smile because, true to form, Nash hadn't liked Robin at first either. He'd been ten and Robin twenty-two and fresh out of agricultural college. In his defense, he had given Burl the stink eye too.

"Fine." Nash sipped at his coffee to hide his frustration.

Robin moved closer to lean against the edge of the kitchen island and directly across from Nash.

"Give him a chance. For me?"

That was unfair. Robin knew Nash would do just about anything for her.

They had terrible fathers in common and in the end that had proved to be a powerful bonding point. Nash's father had come to Twisted Pine when Nash was ten, tagging along after a cousin who was married to Robin's mom for about ten seconds. The start of the best years of Nash's life followed. He fell in love with the ranch and everything about it. When his dad left for the last time, Nash had refused to go with him. His father's promise of finding them a better place was nothing more than a pipe dream. He'd known this even when he was a teenager because there was no better place in the world than Twisted Pine.

His father had never returned. At heart, he'd been a wanderer, unable to put roots down. Even at sixteen, Nash had known he didn't want to spend his life on the road. Twenty-two years in, Nash's roots at Twisted Pine were deep.

"Well?" Robin prodded.

"Fine," Nash grumbled. "Yes, I will give Stone a chance." In his head he added, *one chance*. Max Stone got one chance. If he messed it up, Nash was going to escort him off the ranch and out of Collier's Creek himself.

"Go into town, why don't you?" Robin said. "I don't want to see your face again until tomorrow. Just stop by the Seed and Feed before you come back. Marvin called and said the piece for the baler arrived. And maybe," she added, "you could hunt down Max and apologize."

With a put-upon sigh, Nash pressed on the brake pedal and lifted his hand off the steering wheel in a time-honored country wave as he slowed for the pedestrian crossing ahead of him. The late afternoon sun shone directly in Nash's eyes and outlined the walker's profile. Nash squinted, wishing he had his sunglasses.

He knew that profile.

Max fucking Stone.

Either Max Stone was an excellent actor, or he truly had no memory of the other night at Randy's. Nash supposed that was possible. He'd been pretty drunk and, Nash now knew, not used to the high altitude of Collier's Creek. And as much as he'd wanted to accept all the invitations Max had extended, Nash had been a gentleman, taking him to the Wagon Wheel and putting him to bed.

It had been very *hard* to push Max's groping hand away that one last time and pull the covers over that sexy body. Why did Max Stone have to be just his type? What had Nash done to piss off the universe anyway?

"The hell." This was unacceptable. His cock twitched in agreement.

The universe was taunting him. Max Stone, aka drunk New Guy, aka Robin Simpson's half brother, was right there in front of him, looking even sexier than he had this morning. Sexier than he had two nights ago.

Fucking catnip. Life wasn't fair.

He kept on watching as Max crossed the street, talking on his phone the entire time. Was the man even paying attention to his surroundings?

Dammit. He knew exactly where Max was heading. And Robin had told him to apologize.

It was fucking fate.

Turning the corner, Nash slowly drove down the street and watched as Max pushed into Randy's Rodeo. Was the man a sucker for punishment?

That ass though. Max kept himself in shape and it showed. The fall sun glinted off the salt-and-pepper hair Nash desperately wanted to run his fingers through so badly that he could almost feel the silky strands.

These were thoughts he shouldn't be having. Why did his libido have to wake up now? And why Max Stone?

On the other hand, the neon arrow of the universe also seemed to be telling Nash that now was definitely the time for a drink and possibly to get laid. If the guy would speak to him after how he'd been acting.

If there was ever a time to grovel for sex, it was now. His cock bobbed a bit in agreement. Good to know everyone was on board.

Inside Randy's, Max occupied the same spot at the bar that he had just two nights ago. Randy was working behind the bar again, polishing pint glasses with a bar towel like someone out of a spaghetti western. Where was Clint Eastwood?

The scene gave Nash a disconcerting sense of déjà vu. His stomach clenched and goose bumps formed underneath his flannel shirt as his cock twitched again. Against his better judgement and all the arguments he'd made to the contrary, Max Stone was what he wanted.

Fine.

Wiping his boots on the doormat, Nash took off his hat and rolled his neck before heading toward the bar and the apology he'd promised Robin he would offer. And if his apology led to something else... he wasn't going to fight the universe anymore.

"Vigil. Twice in one week?" Randy slid a knowing glance toward Max. "What can I pour you?"

Max's head jerked and a pair of amber-brown eyes met Nash's.

"Is this spot taken?" Nash asked.

Sexy lips parted and Max's tongue darted out to trail across them before he answered, "Um, no?"

Nash felt a smile crease his cheeks. He enjoyed flustered Max Stone. Was that so wrong? Was it wrong that he didn't want to go through the motions of mutual seduction, he just wanted to caveman the guy back to wherever he was staying and have his wicked way with him? For hours. Until neither one of them could move.

This was exactly why he'd gone to bed last night instead of joining everyone in the living room. It had nothing to do with trusting Max Stone. It was that he didn't trust himself around the man. Something about Max spoke to Nash, made him want things.

For years, he'd been fine alone. Not particularly lonely or actively looking for a person of his own. Two days ago, a cuddly drunk man fell into his lap and changed everything he'd thought he knew about himself. And when life hands you a sexy-ass man, make lemonade. That was the quote, right?

"It is now," Nash said, setting his hat on the bar and swinging up onto the bar stool.

He was rewarded with a light snort from Max. The dim light of the tavern couldn't hide the flare of awareness in Max's gaze. Then something else flicked across his face—comprehension followed by recognition.

"Oh my god," Max said, sounding horrified. "It wasn't a dream. It was *you.*"

"Can I buy you a beer?" Nash asked with a suggestive leer.

Nash stared down at the man spread-eagle beneath him and licked his lips. Max Stone was even sexier naked. Clothing did not do the man justice and neither did the dreams Nash had had last night or the night before.

A blend of moonlight and lamplight streamed through the lacy curtains shielding the room's windows. The light made Max's half-shut eyes appear to glow and his pale skin almost luminous.

"Damn," Nash muttered. "I don't know where I want to start with you."

"Anywhere you like. But hurry it up," Max said, twitching his hips upward.

Nash was horny, but he wanted to linger over the magnificence that was Max's body. This was their first time, and he wanted it to be as close to perfect as possible.

When he didn't move, Max tossed him an impatient glance and snaked his hand down to wrap his fingers around his cock. Precome oozed from the tip.

Max was hard. They were both hard. Watching him, Nash's cock twitched and pulsed, demanding he hurry the fuck up.

"Hurry? Why would I want to hurry?" he teased anyway.

With an evil smile, Max released his cock and reached for Nash's, stroking one long finger from tip to balls. Nash shivered. Shaking his head—*no way*—he knocked Max's hand away. Nash would be the man in the driver's seat tonight.

"Still not gonna hurry. After not doing what I wanted to do the other night? Not hurrying."

"Maybe... less talking and more doing then? Put your tongue to good use? Just a suggestion."

"Is this how you motivated your employees?"

"Is this how you walk someone back to their bed-and-breakfast?"

Nash grinned, showing teeth. "Not often, but when I do walk a man back to his room, I do it right."

Max's smile glittered in the ambient light. "All this darn talking. Who knew cowboys liked to gab so much? Maybe less talking and more body language."

Nash groaned, wanting to resist the laughing man below him, to tease him a little longer and draw the whole thing out, but really what Nash desired was to taste, touch, and feel Max Stone. With little finesse, he scooted backward on the bed and leaned down, lifting Max's cock so he could wrap his lips around him.

"Ahhhh," Max groaned, arching off the bed and pushing his cock further into Nash's mouth. Max's hands landed on his head, scrabbling for purchase, for something to hold on to. Nash thought maybe he needed to rethink keeping his hair short.

Nash took his cock as deep as he could. Unfortunately, he did have a gag reflex but he did his best. Underneath him, Max panted and groaned, his body trembling under Nash's ministrations. He sucked harder for a moment, and Max's fingertips dug against his skull.

"Fuck, fuck, fuck," he moaned. "Please…"

Instead of answering—Nash figured the word wasn't a plea, just an expression of need—he plunged his nose into Max's crotch and breathed in his very essence before tracing the shape of Max's sac with his tongue.

"Holy fucking fuck," Max gasped out. "I just—"

If the man could speak, Nash needed to work harder. Opening his mouth wider, he took Max's rock-hard balls into his mouth and reveled in the feel of them, in his musky scent, and in the way Max jerked helplessly beneath him. With his free hand, Nash wrapped his fingers around Max's cock again and began pumping. Not hard and fast, just enough to render Max speechless.

The room had a chill to it, but they were both molten hot. A bead of sweat dripped down Nash's cheek, followed by another. He wanted to pleasure this Maximillian Stone who had Nash thinking thoughts he shouldn't be. Like his rules about hooking up with cuddly millionaire strangers.

Rules, what rules? What did rules have to do with Max?

Nash's fingers were slick with Max's precome. Releasing Max's cock and balls, Nash took him into his mouth again, wanting to memorize his taste.

"Nash."

Now his name was a plea. Reluctantly, he swirled his tongue around Max one last time and let him slip out from between his lips. Max was beautiful lying in the moonlight, his limbs taut with want yet loose with abandon.

"One sec."

Nash grabbed his wallet off the nightstand, opened it, and took out the condom and lube he had stashed away. Ripping the package open, he quickly rolled it on, wishing for once he could go bare. Condoms were old school, but so was he. He and Max hardly knew each other and this was not the time for an *are you safe* convo; a man at the end of his rope would say anything.

He tapped Max's thigh. "Turn over."

Max shook his head, his hair curly and wild, the silver threads glinting in the diffused light of the room. "On my back."

Jesus, the man was going to kill him, but Nash discovered he couldn't say no. He would figure that one out later.

"Go gentle on me," Max murmured as Nash kneeled and lifted Max's hips upward. "It's been a while."

Tearing open the tiny packet of lube, Nash spread the slick over his fingers before sweeping them across Max's hole.

"Believe it or not, I don't do this often," Max asserted with a pant.

A surge of jealousy took Nash by surprise. He didn't want to hear about any man who may have had Max before him. Tonight, Max Stone was his.

"Now who's talking too much?" Nash punctuated his remark by pushing his index finger inside Max's body.

"Oh, god, yeeees," the older man gasped, throwing his head back as he drew his legs up and pushed down on Nash's finger.

An ass man, Nash's fucking dream come true.

Max writhed beneath Nash as he added another finger and pushed further inside him. He was definitely an ass man. They were both dripping precome, and Nash did his best not to worry about what Delores was going to think when she cleaned the room. Maybe they could leave the windows open.

"Nash, Nash, Nash," Max chanted as Nash pushed his fingers closer to and then finally directly across his prostate, that little bundle of nerves hidden away.

"You want to come like this?" Nash asked as more sweat dripped down the side of his face. He was close too. Just watching Max was a massive turn-on.

"Can't... don't..."

Nash had no idea what those words meant. Max's cock was flushed red and pointing at his abs—he was very close. Making an executive decision, Nash gently withdrew his fingers and positioned himself at Max's inviting hole.

Without any more words, he circled and then tapped Max's entrance before pushing inside. They both groaned. Max arched his back again and Nash slipped further inside until he was fully seated.

"Okay?" he asked.

Max nodded with what Nash suspected was impatience. He began to move and instantly knew he'd been right. Max was perfect and neither of them were going to last much longer.

He lost track of time, of everything, pushing his hips forward and pulling back again, over and over, giving and seeking pleasure, all while Max had his legs wrapped around Nash's hips, holding Nash's thighs in a bruise-inducing grip.

Nash's already hard balls tightened further and the spark of lightning he'd been fighting off threatened. Before he released, Max threw his head back and come arced from his erection. Nash wanted to watch, he wanted to, but his orgasm slammed into him, so instead of watching Max, he was filling the condom with his own hot come.

Underneath him, Max shook and groaned again before collapsing back onto the sheets. Nash's heart pummeled the inside of his chest. He lowered himself so he lay partially on top of Max. Now that they were still, the chill of the room was making itself known.

Max flailed one arm around, grabbed the comforter, and threw it over both of them.

"Okay?"

Nash nodded. "Okay."

His heart did another weird thump. He wasn't sure if he was okay or not. What the hell had that been? Since when did he take relative strangers—who he wanted to distrust—to bed and fuck the dickens out of them?

Did he actually *like* Max Stone?

Was it possible he was totally fucked? Max Stone was in town for one reason—Twisted Pine Ranch. Not for Nash Vigil. Soon enough he'd leave, Nash reminded himself. Just like Craig Stone had. Just like Nash's father had.

NINE

Max

"You should cancel your reservation and stay out at the ranch," Nash said.

Max eyed his—well, whatever Nash Vigil was to him after a night like the one they'd had—with suspicion and the tiniest glimmer of hope.

"No offense, but just two nights ago, you were giving me the arctic shoulder."

He was still processing the fact that the man who'd tucked him in at the Wagon Wheel was none other than Nash Vigil. Nash was the shadowy man he'd been unable to remember. Unable to forget either. Deep down, he'd known him though; his primal brain had been on duty.

"Is that colder than a cold shoulder?"

Little snippets of memory kept coming back to him now, like not being able to resist setting his hand on Nash's thigh. God, what a drunken idiot. He was damn lucky. And more than a little shocked at his behavior. He never did anything like that.

"Yes, absolutely," Max confirmed, nodding very hard. "Very,

very cold."

Sighing, Nash rolled onto his side to face Max.

"You took me by surprise," he complained. "Twice! First when you were all sexy and drunk at Randy's and I had to be the bigger person and keep my hands off you. Then on the road the next day? Look, I'm sorry for my behavior. But, dammit, I'd spent the entire night wondering if I'd made the right decision leaving you. And, when I finally got to sleep, there you were again." He scowled. "It'd been a long time since I woke up with an aching hard-on and had to knock one out in the shower."

"And then I didn't remember you," Max pointed out.

There was Nash's sexy scowl again. "Exactly! How could I possibly be forgettable?"

Nash Vigil was not forgettable at all, and that worried Max. It had only been a few days since he arrived in Collier's Creek and he already wasn't looking forward to saying goodbye when it came time for him to go. After he'd completed his mission and Twisted Pine was out of financial trouble, of course.

"To be honest," Max said, "I kept thinking you seemed familiar. It was driving me nuts."

"Yeah, yeah, sure." Nash said wryly, pointing at himself. "This is the kind of face that could be anyone's."

"Hm, nope," Max replied as he gently pushed Nash onto his back. "Not anyone."

Once they resurfaced twenty minutes later, give or take a few, Nash brought up the ranch again.

"Robin invited you to stay there. You should take her up on it."

Max was learning what it felt like to be boneless. How could Nash even think right after sex? And hadn't Nash made his animosity toward Max's presence on the ranch clear, regardless of how awesome the sex was?

"Hm, but don't you think I'm out to take over the ranch with all my buckets of money?"

Max had finally figured out that was exactly what Nash had thought before meeting him. Still thought. Possibly.

Nash's cheeks reddened. "I might have thought that before. But not now."

"What do you think now?" Max fished.

"I think it would be nice to have you out at the ranch so you and Robin can get to know each other better... and we can too." He held up a hand to stop Max from saying anything. "That's all it will be. Getting to know each other, having a good time while you're here. I'm fully aware you won't be staying, but there's no harm in having a good time."

Robin's smiling face popped into Max's head. He liked his older half sister, and he did want to get to know her better.

His brother claimed Max had abandonment issues and that was what drove him to make the trek to Collier's Creek, but Max disagreed. He'd never wished for a cookie-cutter family. Robin and her mother had truly suffered when the asshole known as Craig Stone had decided to fully leave Wyoming and start a new life on the West Coast. He'd cleaned out the family bank accounts and disappeared. Creditors had come in fast and furious, but Robin's mom hadn't had any resources.

Yes, something similar had happened to Max, Xavier, and their mom Wanda when Craig Stone had pulled the same disappearing act on his second family. But as Wanda liked to point out, they hadn't had a lot to steal in the first place and all the accounts had been in Wanda's name because presumably Craig was trying to lay low. She'd felt like an idiot for not suspecting anything.

"Keeping up with you two was about all I could handle," Wanda had said when Max brought up the touchy subject.

Life had been rough for a while but they'd made it. Max never had tried to find his bio father but suspected he'd headed somewhere remote like Alaska, where it might have been easier to create an identity, and he figured there was at least a one more family out there somewhere, one more woman Craig had conned and lied to. Hopefully no kids.

"What about Robin?" he asked. Did they want her to know they were "getting to know each other"? Max wasn't sure.

Nash pursed his lips. "We're adults. We're not doing anything wrong or breaking any laws. I would never ask you to hide anything."

"I don't want to hide anything... I just"—he shrugged—"want to savor the moment? Does that make sense? I have the feeling Robin would be all up in our business."

"She means the best, but you're not wrong," Nash said. "Robin's been trying to set me up with eligible bachelors around Collier's Creek since I was eighteen. Once she even tried to set me up with JD." The last was finished with a shudder and a grimace.

"Who's JD?"

"Nowadays, he's the sheriff. Back then he was the Collier's Creek equivalent of a beat cop. Don't get me wrong, JD's a good enough guy. He's just not my type."

"And a nerdy ex-software guy is?" Max questioned. "I think you need your head examined."

Robin was ecstatic at Max's change of mind. When he arrived the next day, she immediately put Max in the same room he'd slept in the first night.

"Dinner's at six!" Her gaze landed on Nash, who'd been working at the computer in the kitchen. "The sun is still shining so Nash can give you a tour before then."

Max suppressed a grin. Robin must have thought she was forcing Nash to be nice to him. If she only knew.

"I have time now," Nash said, rising to his feet. "We'll start with the barns."

.   .   .

Long past dinner, after the fireside chat and after the house lights had been turned off, a light tap sounded on Max's door. *Tap-tap, tap, tap-tap*. Their predetermined code. Max felt like a naughty teenager.

Naked and half-hard already, he swung his legs off the bed and crossed to the door. Nash waited in the hallway, wearing only pajama bottoms. With an appreciative waggle of his eyebrows, he pushed past Max into his room. Almost before Max had the door shut and locked, Nash had stripped down to nothing.

"Let's get started with the rest of the tour," Nash said.

"You've never ridden a horse?" Robin's brows drew together like Max not riding a horse was the most astounding fact she'd ever heard.

He'd been at the ranch for two weeks already, alternating between following Nash around, shadowing Robin, and spending his free time binge-reading the ranch's tattered Louis L'Amour collection.

Inadvertently, he'd learned quite a bit about how an operation like Twisted Pine worked, as well as just how much depended on chance. If the weather was bad, or the stock got sick, or a natural disaster occurred, they could easily go under. Max didn't want that to happen.

"Not really. Does Keilly Carson's eighth birthday party count?"

"Were you also eight?"

Max nodded. "And nine. Ten too. But after Xavier and his friend Forrest stole her lunch one year and replaced it with a grass sandwich, we weren't invited again."

He'd never understood why they'd decided on a grass sandwich or what had provoked the theft in the first place. As kids, Xavier and Forrest Cooper were like electrons that bounced off each other, gathering more energy every time they did so until they were both grounded for a few days. Then it would start all over again. He'd always felt sorry for Forrest's grandfather, who seemed to spend most of his days in the school principal's office. Their mom ran her own business though and couldn't just run to school at the drop of a hat. She'd claimed Grandpa Cooper had her on speed dial.

"Then, no, it doesn't count," Robin confirmed. "But at least you've been around them."

They were standing in the barn where the horses were kept. Stabled? Max was going to need to learn horse lingo if he was going to stick around.

"It's fine. I don't really feel like I missed out on anything. Software engineer, not cowboy."

Stick around? What the hell was he thinking?

An hour or so later, Max shouldn't have been so surprised at finding himself being unceremoniously hoisted onto the back of a giant mammal. But he was. And nothing he said dissuaded Robin or Nash.

"Jesus Christ, they have huge teeth." He whispered the words, as if the horse was listening to him.

"Buttercup wouldn't hurt a fly," Robin said. "She hardly likes to trot, much less anything faster. We always tell folks she's like riding a couch. A very comfortable couch."

Max stared down at his half sister. Amusement glittered in her eyes as she smiled back up at him. Damn, the ground seemed very far away from where he was sitting. Buttercup shifted underneath him and Max grabbed the pommel to keep from falling off. Luckily, Nash had turned away. Robin pursed her lips together.

"Let's do a trial run before you head out."

She led Max around the training yard a few times and then had him go on his own while she sat on the fence and watched.

"This is ridiculous," he muttered, still not sure how he'd been convinced. Possibly Nash had promised him a blow job later on.

"Nash will make sure you're fine." She patted his thigh. "You don't need to keep the pommel in a death grip. Just hold the reins lightly in one hand and let Buttercup take care of you. She's very good at her job."

Max glanced over at Nash, who was returning to the pen and leading a huge, saddled, brownish-colored horse out of its stall. The horse's hide was glossy and looked well-groomed, not a surprise when it came to Nash. The two of them together reminded Max of an old-timey cowboy painting; all they needed was a dramatic background. What was he thinking? They already had a dramatic background.

While he sat on Buttercup like a sack of potatoes, Nash vaulted onto Ricardo with the grace and ease of a lifelong rider. Because he *was* a lifelong rider. This did not make Max feel any better about being a newbie.

"Show off," Robin muttered, smiling at Nash. "He could probably ride before he could walk, he should be an excellent horseman."

Max smiled back, secretly pleased that Nash Vigil might want to impress *him*.

"We're only going up to the top of that hill and back," Nash said over his shoulder. "Nothing to worry about. Buttercup's done it a million times."

Max was sure there was something he should be worrying about, like which hill Nash had been referring to. But watching Nash on his horse had his concerns melting away like ice cream on hot pavement. Nash had made him watch several videos the night before, and again this morning, on how to hold reins and basic horseback riding. And Max had already proved he knew how to steer right and left during his quick lesson with Robin, even though Buttercup responded so slowly it was hard to tell if she was awake.

Robin cleared her throat. Swinging his focus back to his half sister, Max realized she'd been watching him watch Nash. Winking at him, she waggled her eyebrows as she glanced at Nash, mouthing, "I approve."

Max's face burned. At least, he hoped that's what she'd said. The fact that he and Nash were not nearly as sly as they thought they'd been was truly mortifying.

The horses clearly knew where they were going. To Max's untrained eye, they appeared to be heading randomly west-ish. But after a quiet twenty minutes, he realized they were tromping along a crease in the hillside and slowly gaining elevation. He also realized that "just to the top of that hill" wasn't that close. Distances were deceptive at high altitudes.

"You doing okay back there?" Nash asked over his shoulder.

"Great," Max called back. He would never admit it if he wasn't, but he *was* doing great. Tonight he would want to soak in a hot bath for sure. Maybe Nash would soap him up? His cock twitched at the thought. Ten feet off the ground was probably not the best place for an erection.

He forced his attention away from Nash.

The day was crisp but bright, and the few deciduous trees mixed in with the stands of pine trees were showing off their reds, oranges, and yellows. Max had borrowed a fleece-lined jacket from Burl but left it hanging open for the time being. It was warm enough now, but he'd learned the hard way that the weather changed quickly around here. However, with the sunshine today, it was warmer than he'd expected.

"Eventually, this trail would take us up to the high pastures, the ones we use in the summer." Nash's voice drifted back to him. "But the stock has already been brought down."

"Nice. So no rodeo roundup for me."

"Nope. If you're here when summer comes around again, you should go on one of the rides. Guests seem to love them."

"Maybe." He didn't want to think about leaving and he really wasn't ready to think about next year. For once in his life, Max was relishing the immediate, the now. The *today*.

They fell into another comfortable silence. The only sounds were of the horses' hooves clomping against the dirt. High above them a bird of prey circled, searching for its next meal. Every once in a while, it let out a long shrill call that sent shivers down Max's spine. A few late-season crickets leaped high and clicked in alarm as they began to cross an open grassy area.

He could get used to this, Max thought. But he wouldn't allow himself to. Nope, nope, nope. A sexy cowboy was not the reason he'd come to Twisted Pine. Still, Max found himself sniffing the fresh air and the earthy scents it carried to his nose, memorizing them. And, of course, continuing to watch the man in front of him.

Nash's strong shoulders were currently protected by a waist-length denim jacket, and Max wanted to peel it off him slowly and then move on to the long-sleeved shirt he wore underneath. Max knew what he wore because he'd watched Nash pull the shirt over his head before the sun rose that morning.

So, yeah. They weren't being all that sneaky, but Robin seemed to be the only one who'd caught on. He couldn't imagine that the brothers would be at all subtle if they knew. Burl though?

Maybe Burl knew too.

Max was half paying attention to Nash in front of him and half paying attention to nothing. The hawk flying overhead made a tighter circle as it spotted something, and Max was watching it change its wing formation when a crack and odd whiffling sound caught him by surprise. It felt right next to his ear, a weird whooshing sensation. Instinctively, he jerked away from whatever it was, his borrowed cowboy hat falling to the ground.

Buttercup, who, he'd been assured several times, was supremely unflappable, squealed and leaped sideways before galloping up the path as if she were being chased by the hounds of hell. The reins were useless. They'd been jerked from his fingers when she bolted, forcing Max to grab at the pommel and her thick mane in order to keep from falling off.

Max finally managed to get his fingers around the strands of leather but, fucking hell, pulling on the straps didn't seem to do anything. His boring life flashed before his eyes as Buttercup kept moving, kept running away from Nash and Ricardo.

He thought he heard Nash yelling, but Max had no idea what he was saying. It was all he could do to stay in the damn saddle and not be tossed to the ground.

"Whoa, whoa!" He hauled on the long leather straps again, but his grip was poor and Buttercup still wasn't slowing down for anything. All Max knew for sure was that his back and ass were going to hurt like hell and sooner rather than later. But, he decided, he'd rather have a sore back than be tumbling down the hillside.

The pretty scenery was a blur. Had they stayed on the trail or had Buttercup decided ranch life was too hard and she was making a run for the border? Maybe Canada? Wasn't Montana in the way?

From behind him came shouting again. He hoped it was Nash and not some ghost-cowboy out for his revenge. Still, there was nothing he could do to get Buttercup to stop or even slow down; she was heading for the faraway hills Nash had pointed out earlier and Max was holding on for his fucking life.

It felt like hours passed with nothing but the thundering sound of the horse's hooves against the earth—more likely it had only been a few minutes of abject terror—when Buttercup finally began to slow her pace. She seemed to stumble a bit before slowing to a walk, her sides heaving against his legs.

"Whoa, girl," he said uselessly, patting her neck. She was a sweaty mess and Max's heart was about to thunder out of his chest.

"Hold on, Max! Hold on!"

Of course he was fucking holding on. He also wasn't going anywhere that didn't involve using his own two feet for the rest of his life.

The fact he was still in the saddle was a miracle. Max couldn't bring himself to pry his fingers from the pommel and dismount. Instead of dismounting, he stayed where he was, trembling and thanking his guardian angel he wasn't lying somewhere along the trail with a broken neck or other injury.

Or dead. He easily could've been dead.

"Fucking hell," he whispered. His voice was shaky and weak. "What the fucking hell was that about?" Sweat dripped down his face and between his shoulders, making him shiver with cold now that he wasn't holding on for dear life.

With a clatter of hooves, Nash was pulling up next to him. Reaching over, he tugged the reins out of Max's vice-like grip. Nash's expression was grim as he slipped to the ground and closed the distance between them.

"What the fuck happened?" Nash demanded as his hand landed on Max's thigh. The light touch took him down a notch.

"I don't know," replied Max shakily. "I have no idea. One minute I was... watching the view ahead of me, and the next, she was running and it was all I could do to stay on the damn horse." He glanced around, wondering where the hell they were. "Where are we?" he asked.

"We're definitely not where I planned for us to be," Nash bit out. "But there's an outbuilding up here that we sometimes use in the summer to store stuff for the cattle drives. We'll go up there and I'll check out Buttercup and make sure she's OK. I've never heard of her doing anything like this before. You really are okay?" Nash's intense gaze met Max's. "It was you I was worried about. I love Buttercup and all, but if you'd fallen off that horse..."

my fucking life flashed before my eyes." He raised an arm. "Let's get you down. Buttercup is hurt."

"Your fucking life? Try mine. It played out repeatedly. And the only thing I learned is that I'm boring." Under his breath, he muttered, "And damn, Xav was right again."

Max's pride wanted him to gracefully dismount, but it was all he could do to swing his leg over and slide out of the saddle into Nash's embrace.

Nash grabbed him before Max fell to his knees and buried his face in Max's neck. Max leaned in, relishing being alive and unhurt, his arms tight around Nash's waist.

"Fucking hell," Nash murmured, the brush of his lips tickling Max's neck. "Don't scare me like that again. You only just got here. I just—" He didn't finish the sentence, just shook his head at what hadn't happened.

Blinking, Max dredged up the willpower to try and reassure Nash, even though his heart rate had barely slowed. If Nash's life had flashed before his eyes, Max's had played out in full Dolby surround sound.

"I'm okay," he managed. "I'm, I think I'm fine. I just don't know really how much I want to get back on the horse."

Nash pulled away and began to circle Buttercup, bending to run his hands along each sturdy leg. Max shuffled after him.

"She's been wounded," Nash said grimly, looking up at Max. "I think that graze is from a bullet."

"As in with a gun?"

"Shot, as in with a gun," Nash confirmed, pointing to a deep gash in her flank. "I think so anyway. There was nothing on the trail that would leave a mark like this."

"Why? Who would do something like that?"

Scowling, Nash rose to his feet. He lifted his hand and then seemed to realize his hat was no longer on his head.

"No idea, but we need to get Buttercup looked at."

TEN

Nash

"I agree, that's likely a bullet wound," Kit Larson said grimly, anger morphing his usually gentle expression into something that boded danger for the shooter if he ever came across him. "See how it starts here with a darker mark and gets wider? The narrow spot is where it first hit and then it gets wider as it scraped along her hide."

Kit was one of two large animal veterinarians who served the Collier's Creek community. In his early sixties, he was bald on the top and sported a gray fringe that always seemed to need a trim. Animals loved him, and so did humans.

Nash had called the vet while he and Max rode Ricardo back to the ranch, slowly leading the injured Buttercup, and Kit had been waiting there for them when they arrived. Nash probably didn't want to know what laws the vet had broken to get to Twisted Pine so quickly. He would've liked to enjoy having his arms wrapped around Max while they rode, but it had taken everything he had not to scream and rage at the asshole who had taken a shot at them.

"Luckily, it's not deep. We'll give her some antibiotic and keep the wound covered for a few days. Be sure to walk her around the pen so she doesn't get stiff." Kit frowned. "Whoever did this, I hope you find them. We're all lucky it's merely a graze and that she didn't break anything on that run."

She easily could have broken a leg on that unprecedented gallop for the hills, Nash knew. He briefly shut his eyes against that memory and the image of Max lying lifeless on the rocky ground, reminding himself for the hundredth time already that it hadn't happened like that. Max was shaken up but physically fine. He breathed out, searching for a calm he didn't feel.

"From what you've told me, your friend is lucky he was riding Buttercup and not one of the other horses."

"I think so too, although I don't know if he's going to be riding again for a while."

"You know what they say about getting back on the horse…"

"Yeah, yeah, fall seven times, get back up eight. He's a city guy." Nash shrugged. "We'll see."

The smile lines at the corners of Kit's eyes deepened. "He'll be fine. Don't let him dwell on it."

"Right now, I think he's soaking in a hot bath. That was a bit too exciting for his first real ride."

"Robin's half brother, you say?"

"Yep. That bastard, Stone, ran away and started another family, then deserted them too. Max has a twin brother back in Washington."

"I thought he looked familiar. I haven't laid eyes on Stone in decades, of course, but he was a distinctive-looking man. That shock of hair was hard to miss." Kit banged Nash's shoulder companionably. "Well, the patient will recover. Just keep an eye out for infection and call me if you see something. I'll come right out."

"Thanks."

Kit tipped an imaginary hat. "It is my job, after all."

Nash suspected Kit had a bit of a crush on Robin and had for years. Robin appeared to be oblivious to Kit's sideways looks when he was on the property and the fact that his invoices seemed below market. As far as Nash knew, she'd only had one serious relationship and after that guy had died in a motorcycle accident, she'd thrown herself even further into ranch life. Maybe he needed to interfere with *her* love life.

Nash watched as Kit climbed into his mud-splattered Jeep and drove off. The vet's car disappeared from view just as a white four-wheel drive appeared, approaching a bit faster than was safe. Nash recognized the sheriff's logo on the car door.

"Whoever did this is long gone, Sheriff," Nash said wryly after walking him into the barn to show him Buttercup's injury and describe where he and Max had been riding. "No need to break the sound barrier like Larson did."

A few years older than Nash, JD was a handsome man with craggy, weatherworn cowboy looks. JD was also related to the town founder—Jacob Collier—so his name held cache in town. Nash didn't think his genealogy stopped crime, but those folks into history liked meeting him.

"It's all about appearances. Ben—er." He cleared his throat. "The dispatcher said there'd been a shooting?"

Internally, Nash rolled his eyes. Ben Johnson was one of the Sheriff's Office dispatchers. Anyone with a brain in their head could tell JD had it bad for the younger man. Neither of them seemed to be aware of the other's feelings and in fact denied them if anyone was foolish enough to mention it. Personally, Nash found it amusing as hell.

"You think whoever it was might have been hunting?" JD asked.

"Hunting?" Nash scoffed. "On private land? And not just near our boundary, but miles inside our property lines?"

"Had to ask. You didn't see anything?" JD had a little note-book in his hand and a chewed-on gold pencil at the ready.

Too bad Nash didn't have much to tell him.

"I was ahead and then my focus was on Max and Buttercup. I didn't think to look around. Honestly, it wasn't until later that I realized it was a gunshot I heard."

Fear had kept Nash from looking around, as if locking his eyes on Max's back would keep him from being thrown to the ground. Pure terror had coursed through his veins as Buttercup galloped away with a novice rider on her back. Nash hadn't been able to breathe until he and Ricardo had caught up to the runaway horse and Max was in his arms.

JD looked thoughtful as he tucked the notebook into a shirt pocket. "How about you show me where it happened? Maybe we'll find something worthwhile. Then I'll get out of your hair. Do you want to ride with me or drive yourself?"

Nash eyed the faint coffee stain marring the front of JD's uniform. "Did you do that driving?" He gestured at the shirt.

JD looked down at himself and grimaced. "Dammit, no one told me. No, it must've happened earlier."

"I'll ride with you. Save on gas."

It was easy enough for Nash to find the spot where Buttercup had bolted. But JD had been forced to park about a mile away and the two of them walked the path, stopping where the hoofprints suddenly got deeper and then further apart where Buttercup had broken into a gallop.

"Huh," muttered JD as he took in the scene.

"Yep," agreed Nash.

He and Max would have been easy targets as the horses climbed the hillside, the only stand of trees being a few hundred yards to the west. There'd been nothing to protect them but earth and a few random boulders.

"You think whoever it was might have been hiding in those trees?" JD pointed toward the copse of evergreens and aspens.

"Where else?" There was literally no other cover for at least a quarter of a mile. On the other side of the rise, more trees came into view, but where he and JD were now? Nothing. "Plus, we wouldn't be visible to anyone higher up before the top of hill." Just in case JD missed that fact.

JD raised a knowing eyebrow but didn't rise to the bait. "True, true. What's the best way to get over there?"

Nash cocked his head toward an almost invisible path leading toward the trees. Together, the two of them made their way to the woods, Nash keeping his eyes out for footprints or some kind of track. He didn't see anything. The trees' dark shadows inched toward them as they hiked across the rocky meadow. Sunset wasn't far away, and a sense of urgency had Nash moving faster.

He'd watched plenty of crime and detective TV shows, but Nash had never witnessed anyone surveying a possible crime scene in real life. Once they'd reached the forested area, it hadn't been difficult for them to find where the shooter had set up. Just inside the stand of trees was a spot where the earth had clearly been disturbed recently, rocks and pine needle debris moved aside so a human would be comfortable while they waited for Max and Nash.

"I'd say the shooter waited here for you," JD confirmed. "Too bad smoking is out of fashion these days. It would be nice to find a cigarette butt or something."

There wasn't even an abandoned shell casing.

"There's a boot print." Nash pointed a little further away to a spot the changing light had landed on, emphasizing the man-made shape. "And another. It looks like they might have come in from the south."

They followed the scuffled trail of disturbed pine needles and earth until it ended at the edge of another rocky field.

"I'd say you're right. Too bad I'm not Sherlock Holmes," JD said. "I'd already know what brand the boots are, what model car they drive, and how they voted. As it is, I'll have to settle for taking a lot of pictures. There's no one you can think of who would do something like this? You haven't made a new enemy?"

The last was said with a smile, but Nash answered JD seriously.

"I can't think of anyone. I haven't cut anyone off in traffic or stolen a parking spot." Because there was no traffic in Collier's Creek—except on Jake's Day in early fall—and parking wasn't an issue.

Eventually, they returned to the barns. The sun had set but JD wanted to take some pictures of Buttercup's injury. He also wanted to take a statement from Max and speak with Robin and Burl.

Robin must have been watching out for them. When they reached the house, the front door opened.

"Come on inside, you two. I was just going to ask if coffee was in order."

"Sure, why not?" JD replied. "I've already stained my shirt today. How much worse can it get?"

"Someone shot Buttercup?" Harley repeated.

Nash found himself slightly amused at the complete indignation of Harley's tone.

"Our Buttercup? Our loveseat?" That was Radko.

JD was gone, headed back to Collier's Creek. Burl's signature beef stew, which had been simmering on the stove most of the day, was now served up in bowls, and they were all sitting around the dining room table eating a late dinner.

Robin filled Kellen, Harley, and Radko in on what had happened. To say they were stunned was an understatement.

"Why?" asked Kellen again. "Why would anyone do that?"

That was the million-dollar question, wasn't it? Why had someone shot at Max and Nash?

"You haven't pissed anyone off lately, have you, Nash?" Burl asked.

"Why does everyone think it would be me? Maybe it was Radko?"

Everyone turned to look at the young ranch hand. Radko's eyes widened and his mouth dropped open.

"Nah," Harley said. "Wasn't him. Who could hate this face?" Harley grabbed Radko's cheeks and smooshed them together. "Isn't he just so cute."

"Fuck off, asshole," Radko said, swatting at Harley's hand.

"So we've established it wasn't Radko—by scientific method, no less. Nash claims he hasn't pissed anybody off. I'm gonna scratch Useless and Hapless off the list too." Sitting back in his chair, Burl crossed his arms over his chest and stared at Kellen and Harley.

The brothers frowned, looking at each other and then around the table.

"What? Are you not happy to be off the list?" Nash demanded.

"You have a point," Kellen admitted. "But if you need me to take a lie detector test or something…"

Everyone but Kellen burst into laughter, even Max, who'd been quiet since they'd gotten back from their hellish ride. Nash swiped at the moisture on his cheek. Trust Kellen to lighten the mood.

"I don't think we need anyone to take a lie detector test. But thanks for the offer," Robin said once she was able to speak.

"So," Harley said, "if it wasn't any of us, that leaves Burl, Robin, and Max."

"I have to say," Burl began, "any enemies of mine are… old, like me. And not at all the sneaky type. If that bastard Harwood wants to finish me off, he's just gonna drive up in that gas-guzzling Chevy of his. I'll hear him before I see him."

Nash restrained himself from pointing out that Burl's 1999 F-350 needed a gas station all to itself. The Chevy vs. Ford debate would never be settled.

"That leaves Robin or Max," Radko pointed out.

"Since Robin wasn't riding with us, I guess that means *I* was the target," Max said. "Why? I haven't even been in town a month."

"Pshaw," scoffed Burl, still scowling. "There's no way you could be a target. As you say, why?"

No one could come up with a reason anyone would shoot at Max or Nash.

"I mean, just because we've all considered it, especially when you forget to eat, doesn't mean we'd go through with it," Kellen explained.

"And besides, who'd take care of the goats? They're cute and all, but a handful," Harley added.

"Fuck off all of you." Nash showed off his middle finger to the entire table.

Burl leaned back in his chair, resting his hands behind his head. "Anything else weird? Unusual? Dog bark in the night, that sort of thing?"

"Detective Montgomery is on the case," Nash teased. "Burl has a good point though. Anyone notice something odd? Had a weird experience?"

The table was quiet for a few minutes and Nash glanced around at everyone. His gaze skittered past Robin and then returned. Not everyone would notice, but Nash knew Robin very well. She looked vaguely guilty.

"Robin?" Nash asked. "Anything you'd like to share?"

"No." She shook her head. "Nothing."

Nash narrowed his eyes at her. She was covering up something, but he wouldn't press her now. He'd wait until everyone went to bed, then he'd get it out of her.

Out of ideas, everyone drifted off to their after-dinner activities. Kellen, Harley, and Radko were on dish duty. Burl probably planned to catch up on the murder mystery he was reading, but he shot Nash a look and a nod that told Nash he'd seen the look on Robin's face too.

"I'm going to call my brother. I probably should have done it earlier. I'm surprised my phone hasn't been blowing up."

With that cryptic comment, Max headed toward his bedroom. Nash pulled on his jacket and followed Robin to the barn where she was checking on Buttercup. She looked up for a moment as he turned down toward the stalls.

"Oh, hi there."

"Oh, hi there," he parroted, stopping a few feet from where Robin stood. "Spill."

"Spill what?" Robin wasn't looking at him, instead resting her forehead against Buttercup's face and stroking her ears.

"Spill what weird thing you're aware of that no one else is."

"I don't know what you're talking about."

"Robin…"

"What?"

"Burl suspects something too. He was just kind enough to let me come out here alone."

"Dammit. I just don't see how it could be related."

"Why don't you let me be the judge of that?"

Robin sighed heavily and continued to run her fingers along Buttercup's ears. She got a quick huff for her efforts.

"I got an email from Craig a few weeks ago."

"What?" Nash wasn't sure he'd heard her right. "You got an email from Craig? As in Craig Stone, Deadbeat Dad Winner over several decades?"

Now Robin turned to face him. "Yes. I got an email from Craig Stone a few weeks ago."

"Why didn't you tell me? Why didn't you tell anyone? What did he want?"

"I didn't tell you because you and Burl are both hyperprotective of me and to be honest… I was curious."

"Curious about what?" Nash wanted to know. "The only reason he would be in touch with you is because he wants something."

It seemed odd that he would reach out after all these years, and Nash doubted the man had changed for the better.

"That's mean, Nash. Maybe I hoped that after all these years he wanted to meet me. To get to know his daughter."

From the expression on her face, Robin knew this was a fantasy. Craig Stone was a grifter and would take anything anyone freely gave him. And steal everything else. Nash wondered what Max's memories of his father were. It seemed that Craig had stuck around a few more years with the next wife and family. Did Max have birthday party memories? Being tossed into the air as a toddler? Riding a bike? Robin didn't; she'd been less than two years old when he finally quit town.

"Oh shit, I'm sorry." Stepping into her space, Nash wrapped his arms around Robin, squeezing her tight. "I just, I mean, after all this time…"

She nodded, her chin banging against his shoulder. "You're right, of course. He didn't even wait much longer than the first round of emails before he told me he needed money."

Nash leaned back so he could see her face. "What did you do?"

A wry smile quirked Robin' s lips. "I told him the truth. We don't have money and I wouldn't give him any if he was the last man on the planet."

"Good for you."

"After I said no, he told me the consequences would be on my head. Like he's King Lear or something." She laughed but the sound wasn't happy. "I barely remember him. Mom burned all the pictures of him she could find. And now he wants money? Screw him."

Shoving his hands into his pockets, Nash leaned against the stall door and considered what Robin had told him.

"It's weird that he contacted you after all this time. But is his situation linked to some asshole shooting at us? How could it be?"

Reaching up again, Robin stroked Buttercup's nose one more time before turning away and heading back toward the house.

"Obviously, I don't know, but I think it's very weird that he emailed me and not too long after, someone takes a shot at you. This isn't the Wild West." She laughed. "Well, it *is* the Wild West, but we don't have gun wars much anymore. What the hell is happening?"

Nash bumped her shoulder with his as they neared the porch. "I don't know but we need to figure it out. I don't want any of us getting hurt."

"Especially not Max, right?" Robin jabbed him in the side with a pointy elbow and added a knowing grin. "He's good for you. You've been smiling. Radko actually asked if something was wrong with you and if he should be worried."

"Fuck off, he did not!"

Robin was full-on cackling now. "He did!" she gasped. "It was all I could do not to burst out laughing."

"Wait." Nash clutched Robin's arm, slowing her pace. "How did you know, uh, know…"

"About you and Max?" Eyebrows raised, gaze amused. "Unlike Radko, I'm not oblivious to the exchange of lovey-dovey glances between you two… or hard of hearing."

Nash felt his cheeks heat up. "Oh. My. God. Just…" He held up a hand to stop her from whatever else she was going to say. "No. Don't tell me anymore." A thought occurred to him. "You're okay with it? With us? Not that there is an us," he babbled, "but, you know, do you mind?"

He felt off-balance, unsure how to label what he and Max were to each other. Were they a something? They hadn't talked about it any further since Max had come to stay on the ranch.

"Calm down." Robin stopped before opening the door. "I

think it's wonderful. I already told you, I like Max. And who knows, maybe this way he'll really be part of the family."

Pulling open the front door, she stepped inside, leaving Nash standing on the threshold with his mouth gaping open. Part of the family? Max? Was he ready? Were either of them ready?

ELEVEN

Max

For the second time in less than a month, his entire body ached.

Max hurt in places he'd never consciously acknowledged. Was his pancreas bruised? There was no part of him that didn't hurt. He was almost afraid to move, fearing he would groan loud enough that someone in the house would hear him and call 9-1-1.

He'd talked to Xavier for a few minutes last night and assured his brother he was sore but fine, but this morning he was in agony. He hadn't mentioned the supposed gunshot during the phone call, just that the horse had been spooked, thus forcing himself to endure a ten-minute Xavier-style lecture titled *why people didn't try horseback riding for the first time in their forties* before his twin let him get off the phone. Then he'd stripped naked, crawled under the covers, and fallen asleep almost immediately. Nash had joined him at some point in the night. Max knew this because he'd gone to bed alone and currently his lover was spooning him, one arm wrapped around Max's waist.

I could get used to this.

Dammit.

Max bit the inside of his lip. He was already used to *this*. To Nash Vigil in his life. Max liked the grouchy cowboy; he was funny and protective and in many ways Max's exact opposite. But he liked that. He liked Nash's ying to his yang, or whatever folks called it these days.

Max had never felt like what he did was for the greater good. Developing software programs came easily and could change lives, but he'd never been sure the change was for the better.

Nash took care of livestock. He could shoe horses and wrangle goats. There was making of cheese in Nash's future that he then planned to sell at the farmer's market, for crying out loud. Max had also learned from Robin that he'd kept the ranch from being taken away by a predatory lender without taking out more loans. He was a hero.

Max had grown up in a small town, one even smaller than Collier's Creek, but his hometown wasn't as isolated as the ranch was. Then he'd lived in Silicon Valley for years and gotten accustomed to the ease of city life: takeout, more than one grocery store, fancy cars, the multitude of humans crowding sidewalks and roads.

He feared he didn't miss any of it. When he finally left, it was going to be painful seeing Twisted Pine in his rearview mirror for the last time.

This trip had been undertaken with the intention of meeting Robin and helping with the ranch's finances—he still hadn't figured out how to do that without stepping on toes—not meeting the man he hadn't known he needed in his life.

"What are you thinking about?" Nash asked as he snuggled closer, his voice rough with sleep.

Normally, Max would say something meaningless. He didn't share much, a complaint his few boyfriends had voiced. Maybe it was growing up with Xavier, who was an emoter, maybe it was just Max's personality. But after the events of yesterday afternoon and his mundane life flashing before his eyes, he answered honestly.

"That I like it here. And as crazy as it may sound, that I like you a lot, probably too much seeing as it's only been a few weeks. That I have the money to help out the ranch, and I don't want or need anything in return."

He did a quick calculation. Had he been in Wyoming for just three weeks? It seemed much longer—in a good way. Like his soul had found the place Max wanted to spend the rest of his life.

"And, even though my body feels like somebody whaled on me with a metal baseball bat, I actually want to learn to ride a horse."

Before Buttercup had been so rudely shot at, Max had enjoyed the new experience. The creak of the saddle, the clop of Buttercup's hooves against the earth. He'd imagined Nash and himself riding off into the sunset, camping on mountainsides. Who said coders didn't have good imaginations? He didn't want to get back in the saddle tomorrow, or even the next day, but he was going to.

Nash shifted around, gently tugging at Max until he was lying on his back.

"Ow," complained Max.

"I like you here too." Nash's gaze shifted. "Uh, Robin knows about us."

"I know." He smiled. It hurt. "She told me yesterday, when we were getting ready to head out."

"You're okay with her knowing? She's totally supportive, of course, and is going to be such a know-it-all, as if she's the one who got us together."

"I'm okay with everything except my poor abused body. Are you alright with me gifting money to the ranch? No strings attached. I just want to help."

Nash flopped onto his back so they were lying next to each other, his gaze directed at the ceiling. "It's not my decision."

"That's not what I asked."

"Gah." He flopped onto his side again. "I don't know how I feel. I've never had the kind of money you have."

"I didn't until I got lucky. That's one reason I want to share it. But also I have to tell you that my own mother refuses to let me buy her a flashy mansion so there's precedence for refusal."

"Your own mother?"

"Yep, but I sort of got around it. Although I don't think she— or Xavier—has figured it out yet."

"What did you do?"

Max chuckled. "I set up an anonymous fund to support the community of Cooper Springs. All someone needs is to be a full-time resident and have a half-reasonable plan, and they can apply for a grant. It could be for classes they need, a small business loan, whatever." He laughed again, even though it hurt. "Magnus Ferguson somehow got wind of it already and has applied for a grant for the Beach Shakespeare Festival and spring Chainsaw Art Competition."

"The what?"

"You heard me right. Xavier came up with the chainsaw art aspect. The slogan he's currently feeling out is, *Come for the Shakespeare, Stay for the Chainsaw Art.*"

"You aren't kidding?"

"I am not kidding."

"Holy fuck." Nash snorted. "That is incredible. Lead with that, and I bet Robin will say yes."

Max moved to roll into Nash but his entire body seized up. "I'm never walking again, am I?" he complained.

"I think you'll manage it, Clara."

Max frowned. "Clara?"

"From the kids' story, *Heidi*. What did you read as a kid way out there in Washington? Clara was in an accident and couldn't walk?" he hinted.

"Nope."

"Well, Heidi was so cheerful and irritating that Clara learned to walk again just to get away from her. Sorry, I don't have the same disposition as Heidi."

"I accept the Clara role." It was his turn to stare at the ceiling. "Not to complain, but... everything hurts."

"How about I go rustle up some ibuprofen and coffee?" Nash suggested. "In the meantime, you see about getting into the shower. Hot water will loosen up those sore muscles."

Max wanted to ask if Nash was okay with the rest of the folks at Twisted Pine knowing about them too, but that seemed somehow too needy and possibly demanding. He just had to trust that Nash would be honest with him. In fact, he reminded himself, Nash had been nothing but honest. He wasn't the type to hide his feelings.

"Will you be taking that shower with me?" Max asked hopefully, not wanting to overthink what was possibly developing between them. "There is one part of me that isn't sore."

"Probably not a good idea." Regardless of his words, Nash ran his hand across Max's chest, continuing downward and stopping at his semi-erect cock. Max's cock ached, but in a very good way.

"*I* think it's an excellent idea," Max argued. "Maybe not in the shower, but here is good. The endorphins will go a long way toward making me relax." He nodded to emphasize his point and was rewarded with a toothy grin.

"I suppose, if it will make you feel better."

Max's heart skipped a beat. In that moment, Max knew he was in more trouble than he'd realized.

He didn't just like Nash Vigil. He loved Nash Vigil.

It wasn't just the incredible sex, it was everything about him. Even the snarky, grumpy parts he showed most of the world. The realization had been creeping up on Max over the past few weeks, but he'd kept pushing it aside. That damn grin confirmed it though; he'd gone and fallen in love. With a cowboy.

"An orgasm definitely will help me feel better, no doubt about it," he said to cover his fluster. "Maybe that's how Heidi did it."

"How did we arrive at a place where I am about to blow you and we are discussing an alternative and highly inappropriate plotline for a kids' story?"

"This is the unpublished sequel. When they were older, after Heidi was done being cheerful."

"Oh, my god." Nash shook his head. "Since you are able to speak coherently, I'm obviously going about this all wrong."

Leaning over him, Nash gripped Max's cock in one hand and began to employ his talented tongue for the rest of the job. Max managed to repress the groan that wanted to escape his lips, but it wasn't easy.

While Nash sucked, licked, and tortured him with his lips and tongue, Max shut his eyes and let himself drift. He sunk into the sensation and ever-growing urgency to come. Lifting one hand, he gently ran his fingers through Nash's short hair, noting absently that it was longer than when they'd first met.

"Nash…" Max gripped his hair a tad tighter. "I'm going to come."

"Hmmm," Nash responded without releasing him although he shifted his position a bit. Max cracked open one eye. Nash had one hand on Max and the other underneath his own body, his arm moving back and forth.

Holy orgasm already.

Knowing Nash was pleasuring himself while Max's cock was in his mouth drove Max higher and faster toward his release. His hips thrust of their own accord, pushing him further into the heat of Nash's mouth.

"Oh, god. Nash."

Nash sucked harder, his cheeks concave with the effort. Max pulled back enough that he could see the poke of his throbbing hard-as-nails cock against the inside of Nash's cheek. Nash moaned and Max thrust again and then he was coming down Nash's throat, still unable to stop his hips from moving.

"Nash, Nash, Nash," he chanted, hoping somewhere at the back of his mind that the house was empty.

Nash's arm was still moving. Seconds later, his body stiffened and Max's spent cock slipped from his parted lips as warm come splashed against Max's thigh.

"Damn," Max whispered. "That was hot."

Nash slumped against the mattress, the weight of him keeping Max in place. He nodded, unable to speak.

They lay there, panting in a heap of come and sheets for a few minutes. Max stared at the ceiling and listened to Nash breathe. He noted that the house had a quiet feeling to it. Maybe they'd managed to get lucky and everyone was out.

Finally, Nash raised himself off the mattress. "I'll get that shower started for you now."

When Max emerged from the shower, a bottle of ibuprofen and a small glass of water were sitting next to the sink, as well as a fresh towel. After swallowing the pills, he dried himself off and wrapped the towel around his waist before padding back to his bedroom. Nash had been right—the hot shower had helped with the soreness. The pain relievers would take care of the rest.

"Nash?" he called out when he was dressed and heading toward the kitchen.

"In here."

Was it his imagination or did Nash's voice have a more serious tone to it? Moving as fast as he dared, Max crossed the dining room and entered the kitchen. Burl, Robin, and Nash stood around the island. They all turned and stared at him as he came into the room.

"What?" he asked. "Did someone die?"

He was mostly kidding but the expressions on their faces told him something really was wrong.

Robin spoke first.

"Max," she said, coming to meet him. "How are you feeling?"

"I'm fine. What? Is it my mom or my brother?" Why would they know anything about them before he did? Neither Xavier nor Wanda knew how to reach Robin.

"No." She shook her head. "The police are on their way again. Um, Craig was found dead this morning."

"Craig?" Max repeated like an idiot, his thoughts whirling. "Craig who?"

"Craig Stone, our sperm donor."

Of course he'd known that was who Robin had meant, he just was having a hard time wrapping his brain around Craig being dead.

"How? And why are the police coming back here?" Max didn't know how to feel. He'd hated Craig for a long time. And now the man was dead. Thirty-two or so years ago, Max and Xavier had left their house and walked to the elementary school with Forest Cooper and Silas Murphy. When they'd come home, their mom had been meticulously sorting through all the rooms and removing their father's belongings. Wanda claimed their father made the first donation to the thrift shop she still ran.

"He seems to have been killed here on the ranch. Kellen and Radko found the body an hour or so ago," Burl said. "Not that they knew who it was. They called me in a panic and I went up there right away. Can't say I'm surprised, although it would've been polite of him to get murdered somewhere else."

"He was murdered?" Max asked, finding himself unsurprised by the news as well.

Burl nodded. "He didn't shoot himself."

Max shook his head, as if the action might help him sort out his thoughts. "Why was Craig even here? In Wyoming? At Twisted Pine?"

A guilty expression crossed Robin's face. He recognized it because he'd seen it on Xavier's face far too often.

"Tell him," said Nash.

Staring at Max, Robin bit her lips together before speaking. "Craig emailed me."

"O-kaaay?"

"He wanted money."

Not shocking news. "Of course he did."

"I told him no. He said whatever happened to him would be on my head."

"That's a load of horseshit," Burl exclaimed bitterly. "Whatever happened was entirely Craig's fault."

They all fell silent. Max wished he knew what everyone else was thinking. Why had Craig Stone thought he could ask Robin for money? Had Craig known Max was visiting? Had it been his own father who'd taken a shot at him yesterday?

What the actual fuck?

This time when the sheriff arrived at Twisted Pine, several other vehicles arrived at the same time. Nash, Burl, Robin, and Max piled into Robin's practical RAV4 and, with Burl driving, led the response team out to the scene where Kellen and Harley were waiting.

Too bad for the sheriff if he didn't want them all there.

"Twice in two days, I think this is a record," he'd grumbled to Robin when she'd thanked him for coming so quickly.

Max climbed out of the car, ignoring the sheriff's sharp warning of, "Don't mess with anything, dammit." He wasn't planning on throwing himself on the body, he just wanted to know for sure it was Craig and that he was dead. He wanted to see him. Would he recognize his father after all these years? He'd always thought he would, but it had been a very long time.

The years had not been kind to Craig Stone, but Max would've recognized him if he'd seen him on the street. It was a bit like looking into a foggy mirror. Just like Max and Xavier, his father's hair had turned mostly silver early, leaving just salt-and-pepper eyebrows. The general shape of his face, the straight nose? They were the same and Max looked at them whenever he shaved.

It was surreal, seeing his father lying on his back, his blank, unseeing eyes staring up at the sky. His arms were flung wide, almost as if he'd had been getting ready to hug a friend with no idea death was seconds away. A vague memory of his boisterous father greeting someone, maybe a neighbor, with his arms spread wide and a booming "hello" issuing from his lips, floated to the surface of his memories.

"I said to keep back. We don't want you tromping over any evidence," the sheriff said pointedly.

Max moved back several feet and looked around. He wasn't certain, but he thought they were close to where he and Nash had been riding yesterday. But what did he really remember? There were rocks, boulders, and some trees. Lots of dirt and what looked to be rabbit or gopher holes.

"I've never seen a dead person before," said Harley quietly. "Not in real life. Kellen and me thought—well, I don't know what we thought, the guy was just lying there. I guess we both knew he was dead."

Max nodded, his attention on the sheriff's team and the stooped white-haired coroner who looked to be in his eighties.

Nash seemed to understand what Max was thinking. "Not many folks lining up for the job. Aurelio's been the coroner for decades."

"Huh."

They were all quiet, listening to the murmur of the police and watching the coroner shake his head and wave a finger at one of the deputies. There was a chill to the air now and clouds moved in overhead. Max wondered if it was going to snow later.

"Feels like snow to me," said Burl as if he'd read Max's thoughts.

Everyone else nodded and looked up at the sky. Max was secretly pleased that he'd been right.

Nash cleared his throat and spoke. "From a distance, Max and

Craig would look similar. Maybe whoever shot at Buttercup thought Max was Craig."

There was more murmuring and nodding. Max shivered, and it wasn't from the cold. Had someone shot at him thinking he was his father?

"Had the same thought myself," Burl said.

"Or it could've been the other way around," Max said. "What if whoever did this thought he was me?"

"Have the habit of making a lot of enemies, do you?" Burl asked.

"Well, no." He shrugged. "But I do have a lot of money. Maybe they think if I'm dead…"

Everyone was silent again. Burl eyed Max intently before asking, "What would happen if you died?"

"I have a will. My mom and brother are the main beneficiaries. There's money going to several non-profit organizations that shelter those who find themselves without housing, places like that."

And as soon as he had a chance to update it, Twisted Pine Ranch. Now that he knew Robin and the rest of the people who lived and worked there, he knew helping out was the right thing to do. If nothing else, helping separated him from his father. Craig was a taker, Max was a giver, and he never wanted anyone to think otherwise.

"I'm having a hard time thinking that Craig Stone showing his face here at the same time as Max is coincidence," Nash said. "Especially after he had the balls to ask Robin for a handout."

"So… what? He needed cash. I said no. Then somehow he found out that Max was coming and"—Robin glanced at him— "he knew Max was successful. It's no secret, there's tons of articles and interviews. Maybe he thought he could ask him for money too? He must have been desperate. But I have a hard time believing Craig knew Max was in Collier's Creek."

One particularly awkward interview came to Max's mind.

He'd agreed to do it after an incredibly successful program release, and he'd been jittery and nervous through the whole thing. Watching it later, Max had wondered how anyone would believe he could read, much less design software.

"Sounds to me like Craig finally got himself into a squeeze he couldn't weasel himself out of," said Burl. He sounded sort of pleased. Max reminded himself that Burl'd had a front row seat to the consequences of Craig Stone's actions.

Again, everyone's gazes were drawn to the very dead Craig Stone. Where had he been for the past nearly four decades? Who had his father pissed off enough to risk returning to a place he knew he'd never be welcomed again? A thought struck him.

Max turned to Nash. "The first day I was in town, when I went to Randy's." Nash's lips quirked, and Max's ears heated as he remembered how stupid drunk he'd gotten. "When I first sat down at the bar, a guy tried to tell me he knew me. I'd totally forgotten about it. Maybe he thought I was Craig?"

The memory was fuzzy around the edges, but Max clearly remembered the guy insisting he knew him.

"But then I came in and the rest, as they say, is history."

"The rest is embarrassing," Max corrected. "Moving right along," he said before anyone could ask just what history Nash was referring to. "Somebody at Randy's thought I was my dad. Which possibly means he'd been skulking around town for a little while."

"Could've been an old friend," Burl pointed out. "Craig was one of those who collected people like they were Matchbox cars and threw them away just as easily."

"Could've been," Max agreed. But he didn't think so, and from everyone else's expressions, they didn't either. "Do they still make Matchbox cars?"

TWELVE

Nash

Craig Stone was dead. Gone forever. Holy fuck.

The thought rolled around in Nash's head, a loose marble that kept escaping all attempts to lock it away. On the one hand, he was glad the man was gone and couldn't bother Robin, or Max, or anyone ever again. And yet... And yet, Nash also wished he'd been made to pay publicly for his crimes.

Yes, he'd been murdered. That didn't bother Nash one bit. But it had happened on Twisted Pine land. That bothered Nash a great deal. And that fact was going to come back and bite them all in the ass, he just knew it.

"Are you okay?" asked Max.

They'd all returned from the meadow where Craig had been found. JD and Nash's least favorite deputy, Eric Kent, had already taken everyone's statements and left for town. Kellen, Harley, and Radko were heading out again, this time in the opposite direction of the murder scene, to repair some weak spots in the fencing along the eastern property line. Trying to pretend the day was a normal one, Nash figured. He snorted—as if dead bodies were commonplace.

"I'm good," he said.

He was fine, just still mentally picking at the fact that Craig Stone had met his final grisly end too close to home. Nash was more concerned about Max though. He'd been quiet since they'd gotten back and—surprising even himself—Nash wanted to know what was going on in his head.

"I was thinking about going into town," Max said somewhat tentatively. "I'd like to check out the bookstore."

He should do something too. It wasn't good to put off ranch work. This was a slower time of year though. He and Robin had talked about doing a hay run but Nash didn't really want to.

"I should—" Nash began.

"Oh no, I didn't mean I needed you to go with me or anything. I—" Max paused, huffed an insincere laugh, and started again. "It's just that bookstores relax me and I haven't had a chance to peek inside the one here yet."

Nash had been about to say he could put off his plans for the rest of the day until tomorrow, but maybe Max needed some time to himself. He was probably second-guessing his decision to visit Twisted Pine.

"Okay, don't hang around here on my account," Nash replied, feeling ridiculously petty that he didn't measure up to a bookstore. "Robin and I are heading out to check the hay situation in the winter pastures, so we may not be here when you get back."

Ten minutes later, Nash was standing in the living room watching Max's SUV head down the drive and disappear down the rise, same as the sheriff's SUV and the other response vehicles had done. Before Max left, Nash had checked the local forecast again. Snow was predicted but not until later that evening, maybe even after midnight. With any luck at all, there wouldn't be a repeat of a few weeks ago. Nash didn't even want to think about Max trying to drive in another snowstorm.

"Are you ready?" Robin asked as she joined him at the living room window. Her gaze followed his to the empty spot where Max's car had been. "What's up?"

He rolled his shoulders and neck. "Max seemed quiet, wanted to go hang out at Ellis Books. How are you feeling?" Really, the last thing Nash enjoyed was talking about feelings, but he'd do it for Robin. And Max, he amended.

Robin smirked, but Nash wasn't a total idiot when it came to his adopted family. There was a sadness in her eyes.

"Nash, I love you like a brother, you know that. Let's make this short and sweet. I'm mad that I'm sad that my asshole biological father is dead. I wanted a chance to tell him what I thought of him, and someone got to him before I could."

"That's it?"

She shrugged. "Pretty much. It's not like I remember him being here. He was long gone before I was old enough to remember much of anything. All I know is what my mom shared, and that wasn't a lot. But what he did affected the rest of her life. How about we wait until tomorrow to do the hay? After this morning, I need to decompress."

Nash narrowed his eyes. "What are you up to?"

"Nothing, but if you wanted to go into town, you could pick up the harness Cooper Ellis has ready for us."

The innocence pouring off Robin was palpable. Nash snorted. "And maybe stop in at the bookstore too?"

"Maybe take Max on a proper date," she suggested. "Jake's Tap is much nicer than Randy's. Not to disparage Randy, he's a kind person and fine business owner. But Jake's has better food and the floor's not sticky."

"Hey, Coop," Nash greeted his friend as he pushed inside the tiny leatherwork studio in Collier's Creek.

Cooper Ellis looked up from the project he was working on.

"Nash! Great to see you, buddy. How's things? You here for the harness?" He looked over at the wall of harnesses and other leather goods hanging on pegs next to his shoulder.

"Yep, and to say hi. Been a while. How's business?" Nash leaned against the tall wooden counter that divided the studio into a front area for the likes of him and the rest of Collier's Creek and the part where Cooper worked.

The shop was tiny but well organized. It smelled like leather and the oils Coop used to soften and protect his designs. The space was limited on natural light except for the two windows facing the street. Cooper had made up for the lack with several work lamps clamped to his workbench.

Rising to his feet, Coop moved over to the counter and leaned against the other side. "Pretty slow if I'm honest. But it's fall and business is always slow this time of year."

Coop obviously didn't want to talk about the tricky economy that was Collier's Creek. Nash understood. He hated mentioning that Twisted Pine was teetering on the brink of survival, as if saying something would make all his nightmares come true.

"How about you?" Coop asked.

Quickly deciding that if Cooper hadn't heard the news already he would soon enough anyway, Nash filled him in on the past few days.

"Murdered? Holy cow, are you kidding me? When was the last time there was an actual murder? Sheriff Morgan is going to have to brush the dust off his magnifying glass."

"Right?" Nash agreed with a shake of his head. "Nuts, isn't it?"

Collier's Creek wasn't perfect by any means, but Nash was pretty sure that the sheriff and his deputies spent more time on petty crime, speeding tickets, and misplaced property than investigating murder.

"And that guy I saw you helping on the road the other day when it snowed, he's Robin's brother?"

"Half brother. Apparently her deadbeat dad started another family after leaving Twisted Pine. He deserted them too," Nash added the last before Cooper could ask.

"What an asshole."

"That has been the general consensus."

A bell jingled and the door behind Nash was pushed open.

"Nash, Cooper!" It was Geraldine, one of Collier's Creek's more eccentric senior citizens, and she had the pink hair and mop-like dog to prove it. "I'm so glad you boys are here," she said breathlessly. "Barky slipped off his leash! He went down the alley and I can't catch him."

Nash groaned inwardly. The last thing he felt like doing now that he'd picked up the harness was chasing Geraldine's dog, Barkasaurus Rex, around Collier's Creek. The teacup-sized dog lived up to its name, being both vicious and loud.

"Hurry!" she begged. "He'll get hurt, hit by a car, or stolen! Did you know there are people who actually steal dogs?!"

Pulling his leather apron over his head, Cooper muttered, "No one in their right mind would steal that dog. It's a menace."

Nash had to agree. He liked most dogs, but Barky was not on his list.

"Which way did he go, Geraldine?" Nash asked once they were all back out on the sidewalk.

The woman gestured dramatically, causing the sleeves of her voluminous orange plaid wool coat to swing back and forth before nearly whacking Nash in the chin. "That way. He went that way."

"He can't have gotten far," Nash said, knowing no such thing. "I'll head toward the park."

"I'll start with the alley behind my place," Cooper said with a distinct lack of enthusiasm.

Nash got it. He'd planned to already be tracking Max down at the bookstore, and instead he was on the hunt for the town menace. Maybe he was earning some kind of karma points for this rescue mission.

"Hurry boys, it's cold and I don't want Barky freezing. It's supposed to snow."

Tossing the harness into the front seat of his truck, Nash shut the door again and started down the street. Behind him, he heard Geraldine calling, "Here, Barky! Barky, come back!"

Crispy leaves in the last of the fall colors skittered across the pavement in front of him as he strode along. A colorful flyer left over from Jake's Day fluttered where it was tacked to an empty storefront. Bending down, Nash checked under the few cars parked along the street. No killer mop dog there. Turning the corner toward the alley, he paused as the sound of Coop swearing reached his ears.

"Dammit, get over here. Stop that! Ow!" and a quieter, "Knock it off, you little fucker."

Picking up his pace, Nash jogged down the alley to where Coop seemed to be wrestling with Barky. He tried not to laugh but was unsuccessful. Coop shot him a venomous glare.

"You try holding on to him. Here."

Coop held the wiggling wad of brownish-white fur toward him, but Nash stepped back, hands raised.

"No thanks. I'll let you be the hero this afternoon. Geraldine!" he called out. "Barky is back here. Stay where you are, Cooper's going to bring him to you."

"Cooper's going to stuff the rat-dog in the dumpster," Cooper muttered.

"You would never."

Cooper sighed. "I wouldn't. But damn, this beast even puts my love for all animals to the test."

Ignoring Nash's instructions, Geraldine hobbled down the alley toward them.

"Thank you, boys. Thank you so much. Who's been a naughty boy?" she crooned to her beast as Cooper handed him over.

"Let's make sure his leash is clipped to his collar," Cooper said as he did just that.

The two of them escorted Geraldine—and the dog—out of the alley. She waved them goodbye and hobbled off, her vaguely pink hair and orange plaid coat glowing under the late afternoon sunlight.

"Well, that was interesting," Cooper said with a grimace as he wiped his hands off on his jeans.

Together, they watched the older woman make her way across the street, the damn dog proudly leading the way as if nothing had happened.

"I should get back to the shop," Cooper said. "Who knows, maybe someone will drop in and place a huge order."

"I'm gonna head over to the bookstore."

Cooper stopped in his tracks and cocked his head, peering at Nash intently. "Nash Vigil, I've known you for years and have never seen you with a book in your hand."

"Fuck off, maybe I've turned over a new leaf. Besides, I have an e-reader." Which was purely so he didn't have to explain his fascination with gay vampire romance to anyone who lived at the ranch.

Cooper made a scoffing sound—or he suddenly needed a throat lozenge. Truthfully, Nash usually only read e-books, but he wasn't going to defend himself to Cooper Ellis.

"Catch ya later," he said, waving, before he turned away and strolled down the sidewalk toward Ellis Books.

"Say hi to whoever it is for me," Cooper called after him.

Ellis Books was owned and operated by Cooper's grandfather although right now he had some extra help in the form of Logan Nichols. Logan and Cooper were both the same age as Nash and they'd all gone to high school together. They were friends even if Nash sometimes still felt like a bit of an outsider, not having come to Collier's Creek until he was ten. Living at Twisted Pine, he'd been more isolated than a lot of the kids his age too. The upside was he'd never been involved in high school politics.

Thank fuck.

"Logan," he said with a chin nod as he walked past the front desk.

Since he'd already passed the register and was heading for the handsome man he spotted a few rows away, he felt more than witnessed Logan's shock at seeing Nash in the store. Had he ever been inside Ellis Books before? Surely he'd shopped for Robin and Burl at the holidays? They liked to read real books.

The bookstore was what Nash imagined all bookstores should look like on the inside. Dark shelving against the walls was packed with books of all kinds. A few overstuffed chairs were strategically placed for sitting while you browsed and there was a more colorful kids section from where he heard high-pitched voices discussing the pros and cons of flying carpets. At least, that was what he thought he'd heard. There was a unique bookstore scent as well: paper, glue. Hell, he didn't know what it all was.

Max's head was down. He seemed deeply engrossed in the book he was holding and unaware of Nash's approach.

"Hey, sexy, come here often?"

Jerking his head up, a broad smile creased Max's cheeks at Nash's greeting. From somewhere near the front of the bookstore, Nash heard someone smother a laugh. *Logan.* Mentally he told him to fuck off.

"Hey, back. What are you doing here?" Max snapped the book shut and held it down by his thigh. "I thought you were working."

Nash waggled his head. "Robin said to take the rest of the day off. She suggested I take you on a 'real' date. Apparently, Randy's is not her ideal."

"What? I am shocked. Surely everyone loves drunken square dancing."

"I can assure you, not everyone loves square dancing, even sober."

Max widened his eyes. "I'm afraid that you're destroying the image I have of a sexy cowboy. I've also noticed that you don't wear plaid snap-button shirts and often are not wearing cowboy boots."

"Look," Nash replied with a laugh, "you try wearing cowboy boots when trying to catch goats."

"Do I have to point out that they aren't called goatboy boots? Clearly they are animal-specific."

"Tell you what." Nash waggled his eyebrows. "Later on, I'll wear my boots just for you."

"Only your boots?" Max asked in a low voice. "I think I could wrap my brain around that."

Nash had to shift his stance at the image that popped into his mind of himself naked, wearing just his worn boots, and Max sucking him off. Or—nope, he needed to not go further with this or he wasn't going to be able to walk.

"Did Robin have a place in mind for this date?" Max asked, bringing Nash back to reality.

"Oh, right. Yes, she did. Jake's Tap, just a few blocks over. They brew their own beer and have food that's not smoked, grilled, or fried. I mean," he clarified, "they do have all those things, but they also have healthier options. Sometimes they have live music but not tonight."

"So, is this you asking me on a date?" Max asked, a small smile playing on his lips, his eyes glittering with amusement.

"Uh." Nash replayed the conversation so far in his head and realized he hadn't actually asked Max anything. "Fuck."

Max's smile became a smirk.

"Max Stone, would you do the honor of accompanying me to Jake's Tap for libations, foodstuffs, and polite conversation?"

"I hope it's not too polite. Still thinking about cowboy boots over here."

"Definitely not," Nash assured him. The spine of the book Max was holding caught his eye. "What's the book?"

Color flushed across Max's high cheekbones. "Oh, nothing." Max started to slide the book back on the shelf but not before Nash read the title, *The Beginners Guide to Cheese Making.* "Just doing a little bit of research," Max muttered.

Nash couldn't help himself. Leaning in, he pressed his lips lightly against Max's cheek and for good measure ran one hand over that sweet ass. He'd never been one for public displays of affection, but he wanted everyone (and that would mostly be Logan, who he knew was lurking somewhere) to know that Max was his. For now anyway.

"Thinking about cheese, were you?"

"Not anymore." Max shifted his stance too. "But I was. I remembered what you told me about wanting to learn how to make cheese and thought maybe I could learn and help too..." His voice trailed off and his gaze darted back toward the cheese book.

Maximillian Stone was a millionaire, several times over. He was a math genius, had written all sorts of magical computer code, had started his own international company before selling it for an enormous sum and retiring. And now he was thinking about learning to make cheese? With Nash?

"You're constantly surprising me, Max Stone." Nash grabbed his free hand. "Join me for a date?" And if they were accidentally trapped in town that night because of snowfall, so be it.

"So then Forrest and Xavier had to do community service for a whole month." Max snickered. "Picking up trash along the side of the road. Mom was furious."

"I can't see you getting in trouble like that."

Max shook his head. "No way. I let Xavier do all that stuff. It was bad enough people got us confused all the time and thought

I'd been the one who TP-ed the entire high school. Or the time they managed to break into the school office and send a phone message to all the students and staff that school had been canceled for the rest of the week."

Nash snickered. "Xavier sounds like trouble."

"He was so much trouble. Mom always used to say he'd send her to an early grave. He seems to be mellowing out a bit. But then, we're in our forties now, after all. He moved back to Cooper Springs a while back and is selling real estate there. Has a plan to revitalize the business community and the rest of the town along with it. That's where the chainsaw Shakespeare stuff comes into play. I'm pretty sure he's planning on starting something with his neighbor too, but he's playing it close to his chest."

"You guys were close growing up?" Nash found that he wanted to know everything he could about Max Stone. What his favorite color was, movies, books, food. He wanted to know him like no one else did.

"Yes and no," Max said. "We definitely had the weird 'twin connection' you hear about, and we still do. But, as I said, we're very different. I think our dad—er, Craig—leaving affected us differently. Xavier was outwardly angry and rebellious. He wanted to burn the world down and anybody who looked at Mom sideways. I hid away, focused on school and the future. I wanted to get out of Cooper Springs and away from the nosey people who felt sorry for us or judged Mom for not knowing what kind of person Craig was. All I really knew was that suddenly Mom was clipping grocery coupons and for a while dinner was instant noodles or something cheap like that. And that if I wanted to go to college—which I did—it would be on a scholarship."

When Nash had first learned Max and his brother existed, he'd been furiously angry, as if somehow the twins had stolen Robin's father away from her. But the fact was, the blame all lay at the feet of a now dead man. Max, Xavier, and their mother had been victims as much as Robin and her mother had.

"Fucking Craig Stone."

Max stabbed at his salad. "Let's talk about something else. What's your favorite color?"

"Is this a trick question? Blue, of course. I love coffee and tolerate tea. Dogs and cats are both fine. I don't watch a ton of TV but if I do, it's usually action movies, true crime, or detective shows. Things like that."

"Something you've never done but want to."

Nash pretended to think, but he knew what his answer was. He hated admitting this. It made him feel like a small-town hick. "I've never been to the ocean, but it's on my list of things to do."

"I could take you to Cooper Springs!" Max said. His eyes gleamed with excitement. "There's a path right in the middle of town that leads through a marsh out to the beach. It's full of cattails and marsh grasses, and there's an old bridge. There used to be a little resort there too. Not a *resort* resort, but small cabins that families stayed in. Back in the day they must've been cute with tiny kitchens and bathrooms and a killer view."

Nash wanted to say yes, he'd love to see the Pacific Ocean with Max by his side. But surely he was being rhetorical, not actually inviting Nash on a cross-country trip to Washington State. Nash had done a little research of his own. The town of Cooper Springs had its own website, mostly consisting of pictures of buildings in the town and its surroundings. He'd been surprised to learn it was actually smaller than Collier's Creek.

"I mean, not that I'm assuming anything. About"—Max waved a hand between them—"us."

Nash snagged the flailing hand with his own. "I asked you on a real date, didn't I? I don't know where any of this is going either, but I'm not complaining. And I truly would like to see the ocean someday."

THIRTEEN

Max

"When I'm curious about something, I learn everything I can about it. Books, internet research, classes—every piece of information I can get my hands on. That's how I got into software," Max explained. "I just like knowing how to do things and how things work." He'd taken the "teach a man to fish" concept and applied it to everything he could.

"What's the strangest thing you've learned?" Nash asked.

Max shut one eye while he thought about his answer. "A few years ago, my insurance company totaled my car. It hadn't even been in an accident, but the hood had been hit by debris from one on the other side of the freeway. The damage was all cosmetic. I took the payout they gave me for it and that paid for a class I took to learn how to paint cars myself and the stuff I needed to set up a painting space. Voilà, brand-new car for under five grand. I could paint your truck for you if you want."

"Is that why you bought that book on cheese making?"

He'd felt silly buying it with Nash there. And the guy ringing him up had obviously been dying of curiosity, but a quelling look from Nash had stopped him from asking questions.

"It's a start. And why not? I could learn the process and help you out. Surely cheese making could be an exciting second career."

"Max Stone, cheese maker. That has a certain ring to it."

Even though he had been slightly embarrassed—not *sheepish,* he couldn't go there—Max had purchased the book from the smiling bookseller. He was trying to avoid thinking about the *why.*

It was difficult with Nash sitting across from him looking sexy as sin. In the past, Max had mostly dated men in the software industry. They had a similar educational background and were usually in the same economic strata. But Max didn't care about money and most of his dates did. And education was many things, not just a college degree. Money was nice to have and made life easier, but it hadn't been his goal in life to have so much he literally didn't know what to do with it.

And Nash Vigil was forcing him to admit that the men he'd dated in the past were boring, one-dimensional people. They'd never gotten up before dawn to ride out to check on cattle. They didn't have a soft spot for cheese or call a herd of goats a trip. They weren't passionate about much other than their bank account—and Max's.

Max had been dating the wrong men all along.

But... there was the fact that Max was the son of someone Nash hated. Or at least intensely disliked. Nash had made that clear at the beginning once he'd figured out who Max was. He had apologized and even said it didn't matter, but Max still vaguely worried. Would Craig Stone's ghost always be between them?

"What are you thinking about so hard over there?"

"Just me, overthinking. As one does. Especially as I do."

"Nah, you're good at thinking. And other things."

Nash leaned back in his chair. Max found himself slightly jealous of the black Henley the other man wore, stretched taut across his broad chest and clinging to his pecs. His complex blue gaze and deceptively lazy smile pinned Max in place—he couldn't escape if he wanted to. Max met his eyes, definitely feeling a bit like mouse in an open field. A mouse that wanted to be thoroughly ravaged. Nash licked his lips. Max felt a bit dizzy and reminded himself to breathe.

One of the waitstaff chose that moment to stop at their table, breaking the spell. Probably a good thing since public indecency was frowned upon. But what about somewhere much more private? Max wondered if Nash had a connection at the place he'd stayed that first night, murals be damned.

"Can I get you two another drink? And have you had a chance to look at the menu?"

Blinking away further thoughts of sex under a blanket of Wyoming stars, Max sat forward and picked up the menu. He'd already looked at it but his choice was long forgotten. He picked the first thing that came into focus.

"I'll have the brisket tacos and slaw."

Across the table, Nash was still smiling at him. Max's heart skipped a beat. He was very afraid of getting used to this, to Nash's complete attention.

"I'll have the same," Nash said. "And another beer."

"Me too," Max added. "Another beer. But this time I'd like to try the Blackstrap Brown."

The beer names at Jake's came from old mining slang. And yes, he knew that because he'd looked it up. It was all about the research.

The waitperson moved on to another pair of diners, leaving Max and Nash on their own again. Max glanced around, wondering where the restrooms were. He suspected the facilities were through the swinging doors next to the kitchen.

The Jake's Tap decor leaned hard into Old West Saloon style. Big mirrors with gaudy frames hung on the walls as well as behind the bar. There were black-and-white framed pictures of the town's founder and other early white settlers hanging here and there. Gas-style lamps with green shades did their best to light the room, but it was an effort for them. The effect was cozy and pleasant—atmospheric, Xavier would say. While staying at the bed-and-breakfast, Max had learned Jacob Collier had founded the town after discovering silver in the area. The silver hadn't lasted but the town had and it embraced its history to the fullest extent.

His bladder gave him a gentle nudge. "I'll be right back," he told Nash.

The corridor on the other side of the swinging doors seemed darker than the main room. Max paused, letting his eyes adjust before heading down toward the "Cowpoke" sign. A door at the end of the hall, just a few feet from Max's destination, opened and someone came inside. The gleam of a street lamp told Max the door led to the parking lot or the sidewalk.

In the postage stamp-sized one-stall restroom, he quickly took care of business, washed his hands, and checked himself in the mirror. Running damp fingers through his hair, he tried to make the rebellious curl above his eyebrows behave. It did not and never would. He didn't know why he bothered.

Unlocking the door, he stepped out. A man waited there, too close to the door for Max's comfort.

"If you want in, you need to let me out," he grumbled. People were so damn impatient anymore.

Doing his best to squeeze past him, Max was taken by surprise when, instead of heading for the stall, the stranger shouldered him hard. Hard enough that the side of Max's head slammed against the doorframe and he saw stars. The overhead light flicked out.

The man hit him again. Max's face hit the door frame with a

sickening crunch and pain exploded. Instinctively, he raised his hands to try and protect himself.

"What the hell? Stop!" Max shook his head, trying to blink the pain away. Blood gushed from his nose.

"*You*," the stranger snarled, grabbing Max's arm in a painful grip. "What the fuck are you doing here? What did we say about getting out of town?"

There was not enough light coming in from the hallway and with the overhead turned off, Max only had a glimpse of a poorly trimmed beard and thin, mean lips. The cowboy hat his attacker wore prevented him from seeing any more.

"Get off me. What do you want?" Max tried to shake himself free of the man's grip. *What was happening?* "I don't know what you're talking about." He looked again but couldn't see the guy's face in the dim light. A total of six people in the area knew him. This was crazy.

Instead of releasing Max, the man punched him in the stomach. The blow was hard, making Max gasp and immediately feel like he might vomit. He tried but couldn't get enough air into his lungs to yell for help as the man began dragging him outside.

The element of surprise was on his attacker's side and worse, there was no one else around to witness what was happening. He tried digging in his feet but the slick soles of Max's shoes slipped on the concrete floor, and flailing for the door frame didn't work either. The man wrapped one arm around Max's neck.

"Stop, help!" He tried to yell, but the words were hardly a whisper.

A second painful jab in the ribs and more muttered threats were directed at him as he was manhandled out the back door. Fucking hell, he hurt. He was still stiff and achy from the adventure with Buttercup; his body was not ready for this kind of physical onslaught. Not now, not ever.

Max had a brief glimpse of loose gravel and the gleaming

bumpers of a few cars and trucks. He couldn't think clearly or get a good breath of air into his lungs. Why had he never taken self-defense classes?

Knowing how to paint a vehicle was pointless. He wished he knew how to get this guy off him. He'd been caught off guard by the attack, and now it was all he could do to keep from passing out.

He had to try. Steeling himself for more pain, he tensed, ready to throw his elbow back.

But it was too late. A filthy rag or something equally disgusting was jammed into his mouth and some other cloth jerked over his head. He was shoved face-first against the side of a vehicle. Seconds later, cool metal snicked around his wrists. *Handcuffs.*

What the fucking hell was happening to him?

"Don't do anything stupid," his abductor commanded, jerking Max around again. His knee banged against something hard, maybe a car door. Pain radiated and Max thought he might collapse. Then he was being unceremoniously shoved inside.

Panic overwhelmed him now. He could only breathe through his nose, which was full of snot and blood from the punch to the face. He was going to suffocate. Kicking backward, one foot hit something solid and he was rewarded with a grunt of pain for his efforts. But the asshole retaliated by punching him again, this time just above his kidneys, and Max screamed into the rag.

"Get the fuck in. Or I'll just take care of you right here."

He had no choice.

Rope or something was wrapped tightly around his ankles, trussing him like a lamb at the rodeo.

"That should do it," his abductor muttered.

The door slammed and Max was left in the dark.

What the fuck was happening?

Seconds later, the engine rumbled to life and the vehicle

started to move. Max thrashed around trying to free himself—a hand, a foot, anything—to no avail. He was at the mercy of his kidnapper and no one knew. What would Nash think? Surely he'd know that Max wasn't the type to run out on a date?

Was he about to be executed? Why? What about his mom and Xavier? What about Nash Vigil and the beginning of what Max hoped was a real relationship? They'd started off a bit rocky, but Max thought the smoke had cleared. Now he wished he'd told Nash what he was really feeling—love—instead of deflecting. If he got out of whatever this was alive, he wasn't holding back anymore.

The car stopped moving and the engine turned off. Max wasn't sure how much time had passed. An hour? No idea. At some point, he'd lost consciousness. The road had been smooth for a while, but it had turned bumpy and rough a while back. He suspected they'd left Collier's Creek and were somewhere outside of town.

This conclusion did not make him feel any better about the situation he found himself in. Back in the day, when he was CEO of his company, he'd carried insurance for possible kidnappings—always a concern in some places in the world—but he'd never had to use it. And now he didn't have it. Who would want to kidnap him? Especially in quaint Collier's Creek?

The driver had been horribly silent the entire drive. Still silent, he opened his door and got out. Max heard the crunch of gravel as he walked around the car. Max's back ached where the asshole had hit him, and his nose felt like a throbbing blob on his face. Where was Jack Reacher when Max needed a hero?

When he got out of this, he was absolutely taking self-defense classes.

"I'm telling you—*right here.*"

The man was talking, but Max could only make out a few words here and there. He must be talking to someone on his cell phone.

His phone. Hope surged, making him dizzy again. Max felt like he'd been hit by a bolt of lightning. His cell phone was tucked into the front pocket of his slacks. The attacker hadn't taken it away. Hadn't checked him for anything.

That told Max two things.

One, this wasn't a super smart guy.

Two... he didn't have a second one, but thinking he did made him feel slightly better.

Of course, he couldn't reach his phone, so it was a moot point. But there was the possibility authorities could use it to find his body when they finally got around to looking for him.

Max realized he was shaking, either from the cold that was quickly taking over the car or from his injuries. If they left him wherever they were now, the slacks and light sweater he had on were not going to ward off the Wyoming chill for long.

This was not happening.

He'd finally met someone he truly connected with. A snarky, grouchy, sexy-ass cowboy who ticked all his boxes and some he hadn't known he had. When Max got back to the ranch, the first thing he was doing was telling Nash he loved him. He'd been dancing around the truth, but now it was blindingly bright. Why had he waited? What was the point of waiting when you loved someone?

He loved Nash Vigil.

It didn't matter that Nash lived in the wilds of Wyoming. Max would move. He'd move and they'd build a place together. Nash could raise goats and work at Twisted Pine. Max would learn how to make cheese and ride a horse.

While he lay there helpless, shivering, and getting colder and colder, he replayed his new favorite memories—and planned on making more of them. Nash riding Ricardo in front of him, the afternoon sunlight limning his profile. Nash laughing. Nash naked and straddling Max's hips.

No way was this nameless asshole taking Max's future from him.

FOURTEEN

Nash

Nash tapped the tabletop restlessly, their food was getting cold. Max had been gone a long time. Too long. Long enough that the waiter had returned with their second beers and the tacos they'd both ordered. Should he be worried?

He was worried.

Should he check on him? Maybe he had appendicitis and was passed out on the floor—that had happened to a friend once. Max was still sore from his adventure on Buttercup, and Nash had noticed him wincing a few times that evening. But Max was a grown forty-two-year-old man. He didn't need a sitter.

Nash glared in the direction Max had gone in as if he could see through walls. It was a fucking hallway, what could happen? Unwelcome fear had his chest tightening and heart thumping faster than usual.

"Fuck it." Tossing his napkin on the table, Nash headed toward the restrooms.

The small room was empty. There was only one stall and a

small sink. Max wasn't hiding in there. Wasn't passed out from a medical emergency.

"Max?" he called out anyway. "What the fuck? Where are you?" As if the ugly brown wallpaper could answer him.

Max was nowhere to be found inside. Nash pushed through the exit to the parking lot. Not many cars were parked there tonight, not even his. He and Max had walked over from the bookstore, reasoning that Jake's was only a few blocks away.

"You the new doorman?" An older man quipped as he and his —Nash assumed—wife crossed the lot toward him.

"Uh, no. Looking for someone."

"Date run out on you, honey?" The woman asked. "David got mighty skittish before we sorted everything out." She smiled. "I definitely had to do some chasing."

"Really, Lyra? This young man doesn't want to hear about us."

Had Max run out on him? Nash scoffed at the thought. They'd been having a great conversation and Nash had been fairly certain that Max was undressing him with his eyes. And Nash had been doing the same. It was probably good the waiter had come to take their order when they had.

"My friend went to the bathroom. He left his coat behind so I don't think he was planning on ditching me."

"Well, we haven't seen anyone, have we, David?" Lyra said.

David pursed his lips, seeming unsure how to answer.

"What?" Nash demanded sharply. The couple frowned back at him. This was Collier's Creek, not New York City. "Sorry," he said, trying to modulate his tone. "I'm concerned for my friend. Did you see something after all?"

Patience was not Nash's strong suit, not even in the top five. He needed to know what had happened to Max—now.

"Not really," David said thoughtfully. "But when we pulled in, I saw someone helping another person into their car. The only reason it caught my eye is because whoever it was must've been drunk and it seemed early for that. It's not even seven!"

Drunk and not even seven. It wasn't much to go on. Nash had never had a date run out on him before. He was going to assume the worst, that something bad had happened to Max. And Nash knew he hadn't been drunk.

David couldn't say much about the car, just that he thought it was a newer SUV.

Heading back inside Jake's, Nash called the Sheriff's Office.

"You don't have his phone number?" Sheriff Morgan asked again, incredulity lacing his tone.

"Why would I need Max's phone number? He's been staying at Twisted Pine. All I have to do is walk down the hall."

Nash was doing his best to stay calm, and frankly missing dinner wasn't helping. Sheriff JD Morgan asking all these questions when he needed to be out scouring Collier's Creek for Max was pissing him off.

"The hall?" JD smirked. "That's what we're calling it these days? I saw how you were with him earlier today."

"Well, if you saw then you know why I'm worried. Someone took a shot at us yesterday, then Craig Stone showed up dead this morning, and now Max is missing. Something is wrong."

Sheriff Morgan had arrived at Jake's and taken a good look around the restroom and parking lot. Like Nash, he'd found nothing that indicated where Max had gone although he had spotted what looked like drops of blood on the cement floor. A rapid blood test field kit JD carried in his car confirmed it was human. Was it Max's? They had no way of knowing.

The only solid information came from David and Lyra, and the older couple couldn't confirm if it had been Max they had seen or a drunk patron being helped home by a friend. David had allowed that possibly the person hadn't been drunk but instead being forced into the vehicle, but he really wasn't sure. Lyra hadn't noticed anything at all.

"I was busy fixing my lipstick," she offered. Nash did not want to think about the two seniors making out in the pub's parking lot before going in for dinner.

Nash needed to call Robin and let her know Max was missing.

"Duh," he said, whipping out his phone and pressing *Robin.* "What an idiot."

"What?" JD frowned at him.

"Robin has Max's number. She can call him," he said while waiting for her to answer.

"Hey, Nash, I didn't expect to hear from you tonight." He could hear the eyebrow waggle in her tone.

"Robin, Max is missing."

"What do you mean, missing?" Her tone changed to one of concern.

"I mean we were having dinner at Jake's and he just disappeared."

"Were you being nice to him? You didn't say anything horrible, did you?"

"No! I didn't say anything horrible! He went to the bathroom and never came back. He left his coat on the chair and hadn't eaten yet. Can you call him for me?"

He didn't want to tell Robin about the blood, not until they knew for sure. There were plenty of reasons why blood would be on the floor. It didn't have to mean something terrible had happened.

But in his heart, Nash knew something terrible *had* happened.

"I'll call you right back." Robin clicked off.

Nash kept his phone in his hand, waiting for her call back—or Max's. If he'd inadvertently done something wrong, he would apologize and they'd sort it out. Still, Nash couldn't imagine that Max would just ditch him. They were adults, not fifteen-year-olds. And he knew he hadn't done anything wrong.

The screen flashed. Nash pressed Accept without checking to see who it was.

"What's going on?" The voice was Max's but also not. More demanding, with an edge to it that Max did not have even after all the years he'd spent in Silicon Valley. "This is Max's brother, Xavier. Robin gave me your number. Max is in trouble."

Xavier? Damn, this situation was getting weirder and weirder by the second. Why was Max not calling him directly? Why was his twin on the other end of the line?

"He's missing," Nash explained. "We were having dinner and he just disappeared."

"I'm going to make this short," Xavier informed him. "I have a flight out tomorrow morning." Nash started to ask why Xavier was telling him this, but the man just kept talking like a human steamroller. "Max is in some kind of trouble. I've been trying to call him for an hour now, and he's not picking up. We have rules about this, and even if we're not twenty anymore, we both follow them. Luckily, he'd given me Robin's number. My flight lands in Jackson Hole at twelve tomorrow and I'll be in Collier's Creek as soon as I can. I'll call you at this number."

It wasn't really a question, so Nash didn't reply.

"I told him Wyoming was a bad idea," Xavier added. The line went dead. Nash was standing there with his phone to his ear and Sheriff Morgan was shooting him a questioning glance.

"Well?"

"That was Max's twin brother. He's flying out here. He said that Max is in some kind of trouble."

"Did he say what it is?"

"No." Nash shook his head, remembering one of his and Max's conversations. "I think he just knew it. Felt it."

"He felt it," JD said flatly.

"They're identical twins. I guess it's always been like this for them."

They stared at each other for a moment.

"I guess I've heard weirder things in this line of work."

JD's radio crackled to life. Pulling it from the holder, he clicked the button.

"Sheriff Morgan here."

"Sheriff, Mrs. Norman has called in a suspicious noise. She's very concerned and would like you to come and check it out."

The sheriff's eyes rolled upward as if he was asking for patience. Nash completely understood.

"No one else is available?"

"Deputy Kent is on another call, sir."

"Thank you, Ben." He clicked off and tucked the radio away again. "Duty calls. I've got to scare off the stray cat or skunk that's lurking around Mrs. Norman's property."

"But what about Max?" Nash demanded. JD wasn't just going to leave, was he?

"I know you're worried but, first of all, he's an adult of sound mind and body. He may have had a reason for leaving that you don't know about. And second, it's only been a couple of hours. Give him a chance to change his mind."

"But what about the blood?"

"We know it's human, but we don't know that it's Max's. We don't even know his blood type yet. We need more to go on."

JD was worried, Nash could tell. He knew as well as Nash that something was rotten.

"Max Stone didn't wander off. He ordered dinner and another beer. Does that sound like someone getting ready to run off to you?"

"No, Nash, it doesn't, but we need more evidence that something happened. We have to wait. And no, we can't just pull over every SUV in Collier's Creek. Most people in town have one."

JD's answer infuriated Nash, but he was right. They had nothing but some drops of blood and a possible sighting of Max getting into a car. Except, he reminded himself, now they also had Xavier Stone, who was worried enough that he was planning on traveling to Collier's Creek.

What was the common denominator? Craig Stone—and he was dead.

"This has to be connected to the shooting and maybe even to Craig Stone's murder. Isn't that enough?"

"It is enough for me. But we need a direction to look in. At the moment, Max seems to have just vanished into thin air."

Nash wanted to scream at the universe, to roar so loud the heavens shook. But screaming and roaring weren't going to find Max.

"Okay," he said, doing his best to calm himself. "Evidence. Got it."

"Don't do anything rash," JD advised. "Call me directly if you discover something. I am taking this seriously, I promise you."

Just as he was heading back inside, Nash's phone rang. It was Robin this time.

"Did Xavier call you?"

"Yes, and he's on his way here, to Collier's Creek." He filled Robin in with what little they knew. "Can you give me Max's number, just in case?"

"I'll text it to you."

The taproom had filled up with diners while he'd been outside. It was jarring seeing the patrons chatting and enjoying their meals while Max had vanished into thin air. The scene made Nash's stomach hurt. He paid the tab and took one last look around. David and Lyra were occupying a booth close to the table he and Max had been sitting at.

"Thanks for your help," Nash said, approaching them. "If you remember something that might help, would you call me?"

"Of course," David agreed.

He rattled off his number, watching as David entered it into his contacts. Then with a curt "Thank you," he turned and headed back out to the parking lot. He was going to look under every car and every piece of gravel out there until he was sure he'd literally left no stone unturned.

. . .

The pub's parking lot was just big enough to hold twelve to fifteen cars. Less if one was a monster truck, more if they were all economy sized. Long and narrow with only one way to get in and out, it followed the Jake's Tap property line, wrapping around one end in a J shape.

Starting at the street side, Nash used the flashlight on his phone and peered underneath and behind every car and every possible parking spot. There'd been no reason for the sheriff to keep patrons from driving in or leaving, so Nash's hope was that something had been dropped.

What, like Cinderella's shoe?

He was sure the other patrons thought he'd lost his mind. There were definitely some odd looks being tossed in his direction.

"What're you looking for, buddy?" asked a random stranger.

"My other contact," Nash replied sourly after the third time someone asked.

"Okay, sorry. Was just asking."

How to Make Friends and Influence People, the Nash Vigil edition. Maybe he should go back inside and see about getting something to go.

The back entrance opened and then slammed shut behind the questioner. Twenty minutes later, Nash's lower back hurt and he still hadn't eaten. So far, he'd found seven pennies, a dime, and two quarters; one empty purple cigarette lighter; three wood screws—go figure; several tiny springs; a few bread bag tags; and a used condom. Really? In Jake's parking lot?

He was ready to give up when the fading light from his phone caught on something small, black, and shiny. Squinting at it, Nash bent down and picked up the rectangular object. There was nothing on it to tell him *who* it belonged to, but he recognized a thumb drive when he saw one.

Possibly it had been lost days or even weeks ago. But the drive wasn't scuffed or cracked and didn't appear to be damaged—no car had driven over it and it hadn't been stepped on. Possibly it was something boring, like spreadsheets for the feed store. But— Nash turned it over in his hand—possibly it was a link to Max and the only way to find out was to plug it into a computer.

"Come on, Ben," Nash pleaded. "Just plug it in so we can see what's on it."

"I've notified Sheriff Morgan," Ben replied in a steely tone. "He's finishing up with Mrs. Norman now." He glanced at the wall clock across from the dispatch desk. "He should be here in less than ten minutes. I can't believe you just picked it up."

"As if you're going to be sending it to the FBI for fingerprinting," Nash scoffed.

"It's possible," Ben replied haughtily.

"Look, I'm sorry. I didn't think. But waiting ten minutes could mean life or death."

Ben's expression didn't change as he blinked up at Nash. "Nine minutes now. Have a seat. Would you like coffee or something?"

"Are you trying to kill me now? I tasted it once, never again." Nash blew out an exasperated sigh at Ben's stubbornness and slumped into the lone plastic chair pushed back against one wall. The clock ticked ominously above his head, every passing minute longer than the one before it.

Out of pure desperation, he plugged a dollar into the station's vending machine and was rewarded with a bag of chips with a past-pull date of two weeks ago. Whatever, expiration dates were just political statements. At least, that's what Robin claimed. She said if it wasn't meat or dairy to use his nose, not the date on the package.

He'd just ripped open the bag and stuffed most of the contents in his mouth, and was considering calling Morgan himself, when the office door opened and JD stepped inside.

"You found something?" JD asked.

Nash crunched and swallowed the chips before standing up, brushing crumbs off himself as he did so. Ben looked on with amusement.

"Maybe. A flash drive. Could be anyone's."

Ben handed JD the drive. He'd secured it in a plastic bag that had a label of some sort.

"Could be. Let's see if we can look at what's on it. Hopefully, it's not carrying a damn virus or locked up with a password. The entire system was affected by a rogue email last spring and we were down for more than a day. Come on back to my desk."

Nash followed and so did Ben.

JD sat at his desk, plugged in the flash drive, and activated a scan for bugs. The small room was taut with anticipation. When nothing was flagged by the system, he clicked on the square icon that had appeared on his desktop.

There appeared to be several files saved onto the drive. The names were nothing that Nash immediately understood. Little Wind, Shoshone.. Cheyenne, Cody, Sheridan, and Jackson all were towns in the state.

JD hovered the mouse over the file called Jackson.

"Might as well look in this one."

It was a spreadsheet, big surprise. The boxes in the far left column were filled with three-letter abbreviations. SCV, CGS, RNP, et cetera. The next column had boxes filled with dates in month-date-year format, and each date was different. They went back as far as ten years ago and came up to as recent as last week.

"Well, well, well, what do we have here?" JD peered closer at the screen.

Each box in the third column had a sum of money listed. At a glance, the sums ranged from a few hundred to thousands of dollars. Some had been struck through. Many had not.

A few of the rows were red. Some were red with a check mark next to them.

"What are we looking at?" Nash wanted to know.

"Some kind of accounting sheets," Ben said.

JD scrolled down. The last row was 205 and the date was just two weeks ago.

"Possibly," JD agreed.

"It's very simple," said Nash. "The one we use at the ranch has everything and the kitchen sink. This seems like it's just a list."

And nothing on it gave a hint as to what had happened to Max.

"Hmm." JD scrolled back up to the top again. They all leaned closer to peer at the numbers as if suddenly they were going to morph into something understandable.

Ben gestured at the screen. "Could be the crossed-off ones are accounts that have been settled."

Nash stared at the screen, willing something to make sense. This flash drive had to be important. Whoever dropped it was going to be pissed off. Maybe they'd come back to see if they could find it.

"Or could be the crossed-off ones are individuals," Ben said thoughtfully, "and they've paid off whatever they owed."

JD nodded. "You thinking what I'm thinking?"

"Gambling?" Nash said. "Rodeo or something like that?" Gambling was legal at Indian casinos and online. Regardless, behind-the-scenes betting was popular at the rodeos and horse races both big and small. Nash never understood the allure of gambling; he liked his money to stay in his bank account.

A chuckle escaped JD. "I was thinking whoever lost this might be pissed off when they discover it's not in their possession. But I think you're onto something there. This could be a list of bettors."

"The drive could have been lost days ago." Nash steered back to the evidence and away from conjecture.

"Maybe it was. But like you said, it's in pretty good shape if it's been sitting in Jake's parking lot for days."

"Nothing about this helps figure out what happened to Max."

"What did you expect? A map with an X marking the spot? Ben?" Ben's attention jerked from the screen to the sheriff. "Can we duplicate this? Or save it on here?"

Ben nodded.

"Good. Make it so." He laughed at his stupid Picard joke. Ben and Nash just stared at him. "Then I'll take this to Jake's and put it back where Nash found it." Rising from his chair, he grabbed the go-mug sitting on the edge of his desk and brandished it. "I'm gonna need a bigger cup of coffee."

"Don't mind him," Ben said as JD left the small room. "The more worried he is the worse his jokes are."

"So on a scale of one to ten?"

"Eleven."

FIFTEEN

Max

Max was officially freezing. And his entire body was stiff from lying in the same position for what felt like hours, which made everything worse. And he still had no idea why he'd been abducted. At least the cloth was no longer covering his head.

Abruptly, the car door opened. The dome light flickered on, and the dim glow emitting from it seemed blinding after the pressing dark. Max blinked his eyes against it, willing them to adjust quickly. He wanted to see who was behind all this. Rough hands turned him over. Thick fingers grabbed Max's chin, moving his head back and forth.

"What the absolute fuck? You jackass. I *told* you, Stone is already dead."

"Looks like him to me," a second voice said mulishly—the guy who'd attacked him. "He came right out of the bathroom and looked me in the eye."

"Well, look a little closer because Craig Stone was in his seventies—*and already dead*. This guy is definitely not either."

Not yet anyway. Max still couldn't see beyond the light but knew both men were staring at him.

"Well, shit." That was Jackass's voice. "What're we going to do now?"

"*We* aren't going to do anything," said Mr. I-Told-You-So. "This isn't my mess to clean up. Where's the drive?"

There was a rustling sound and some hemming and hawing and throat-clearing as presumably Jackass was looking for the drive I-Told-You-So wanted. It seemed to be taking a while for him to locate it. While they were distracted, Max pushed at the rag with his tongue, trying to get it out of his mouth.

"Shit," Jackass exclaimed, "it's gone. It was in my pocket and now it's gone."

There was a long silence, the kind that Max thought maybe didn't bode well for Jackass. Or himself, for that matter. He worked harder at the rag. He could move it now that he wasn't laying on his front.

"You are a dead man," I-Told-You-So said coldly. "He's going to have you put down like an old dog."

The punch to the head took Max by surprise, but not as much as it probably surprised I-Told-You-So, who dropped like a stone. Jackass grabbed Max's legs and pulled him off the seats. He landed half on the ground and half on top of the unconscious man. Jackass slammed the door shut and ran around to the driver's side. The next thing Max knew, the man had turned his car around and was driving away.

Rolling off the unconscious man, Max wondered why he'd never learned how to break out of handcuffs or untie knots with his toes. If he got out of this in one piece, he was going to learn all this and start teaching classes, maybe start an alternate scout-style group. A hysterical laugh burbled out and the rag fell from his mouth. His cheeks and lips were desert dry. Swallowing, he tried to create enough spit to moisten his tongue.

The other man wasn't moving—yet.

Max wasn't fucking dying here. He was getting back to Nash Vigil and telling him he loved him. That he was in love with him. And if Nash would have him, he wanted to spend the rest of their lives together.

He'd seen it done in movies and on TV. Could he get his hands in front of him and reach his phone? There was a groan from Mr. I-Told-You-So. Max quickly decided that no, he couldn't. Not yet anyway. But he could try and disappear. If he escaped into the dark, the cold might kill him—but he suspected that, if he stayed, the man on the ground *would* kill him. Outside the car, he had a better chance of surviving until rescue. Or at least until daylight when he could see where he was going.

Panic fueled his squirming as far away from ITYS as he could, during which Max realized that the rope around his feet hadn't actually been knotted together. It had just been wrapped around his ankles many times and was starting to come loose.

It was now or never.

Before Jackass had driven off, the car's headlights had illuminated a vista that brought to mind *Children of the Corn*—or worse, *Bone Tomahawk*—which did not inspire confidence in Max's half-baked plan. He still had no clue where he'd been brought to. The why was clearer. Jackass had mistaken Max for his father.

What had Craig gotten himself into?

The only things Max had seen were tall whispering grasses, gnarled fence posts, and barbed wire. A lot of barbed wire. All were ubiquitous to the Wyoming landscape. Regardless, he kicked the last of the rope off his ankles and turned the opposite direction the car had gone, then stumbled into the unknown.

Max had been shambling along for hardly a minute, maybe two, and was barely able to keep himself upright. He needed to get off the road but also didn't want to. However, a shout from behind him had him trying to run.

ITYS was awake again. And even though Jackass had surprised him and knocked him out, Max found this man the more menacing of the two. The fear shooting through his veins propelled him off the road and toward the fence. Once again, he thought he could reach his phone if he could just get his hands in front of him.

"You'll pay for this!" the man shouted.

Max figured he was referring to Jackass and not himself. Hopefully, the man would think Max was still in the car with his friend.

He risked a glance over his shoulder. There was nothing to see. The moon hadn't risen yet, so it was pitch-dark. He was too scared to be cold anymore, or at least he wasn't feeling it.

The sound of an engine starting reached Max's ears. I-Told-You-So had made it to his vehicle. Why hadn't he thought of trying to steal it? It hadn't even occurred to Max that there were two cars on the road.

"Because you can hardly walk, stupid."

Headlights lit up the landscape. Max dropped to the ground, hoping the man hadn't seen him. The earth was cold and wet. He risked another look and guessed he was only a hundred yards or so from the remaining vehicle. After a moment, the driver did a three-point turn to point the car back down the deserted road and Max breathed a sigh of relief. As the car did the maneuver, the headlights landed on a small structure in the distance. Gray and weathered, it could have been a tiny cabin or just a forgotten shed. Max needed to get there.

The moon finally rose, slowly, elegantly, bathing the landscape with an ethereal light. Max would have preferred witnessing the beauty of it from inside a warm house or while wearing an actual coat and gripping a mug of hot chocolate, but beggars couldn't be choosers. The moon was lighting his way and with its help, he only tripped and fell ten or twenty times.

When he arrived at the small building, Max was bruised and aching from head to toe. But he'd made it and that alone gave him a deep sense of satisfaction. He still didn't know what the building's purpose had been, only that it looked to have been abandoned quite some time ago. Maybe it had acted as a shelter for cowboys caught out in bad weather before the road had been built.

Thankfully, the door wasn't locked. In fact, it hung slightly ajar, as if waiting for Max to arrive. He shouldered the door all the way open, stumbled inside, and dropped to his knees. What remained of the flooring creaked underneath his weight but held.

"Christ," Max whispered.

He'd made it this far. Now he just needed to figure out how to get out of the handcuffs and grab his phone. That is, if it hadn't been broken one of the many times he'd tripped and fallen.

For a few minutes, he stayed where he'd landed and listened to the miracle that was his own breathing and the reality of his blood continuing to pound through his veins. The road stayed dark, his abductor having decided by all appearances to abandon Max to his fate.

Well, Max's fate was not to freeze to death in an abandoned cabin. As he was gathering his thoughts, his cell phone vibrated against his thigh.

"Goddammit."

Twisting his arms around, he tried to reach his pocket but couldn't.

Maybe if he stood up again.

His legs did not want to support him but eventually, and with a lot of swearing, Max was upright once more. Contorting himself, he used his fingers to pull his battered slacks around his waist just enough that he could slip his hands into the pocket and pull out his phone with his fingertips.

His fingers were shaking—fuck, his entire body was shaking—but he managed it. The only thing he could do was press Recent Calls and pray that it hadn't been some kind of spam.

The recipient answered on the first ring.

"Max, where the fuck are you?"

He almost broke down and started crying. But he couldn't, he needed to be coherent. He needed Xavier to help him get back to Nash.

SIXTEEN

Nash

Nash wanted to stake out Jake's parking lot with JD but was firmly told to fuck off and stay out of police business, so he took a room at the Wagon Wheel for what remained of the night. He wasn't leaving town until Max was back in his arms where he belonged.

JD promised to call him if anything happened. So when his phone rang, he answered immediately.

"Nash Vigil."

"Nash, Xavier Stone. I heard from Max. He's somewhere outside of Collier's Creek. He said to use this app"—Xavier rattled off a name—"to find him. He doesn't know where he is."

"Is he okay?"

"He says he's cold and tired but generally okay. He's lying. He's scared and freaked the fuck out. Hang up and find my brother. His phone is low on battery, so don't waste any time. I'll call you when I get into town."

Xavier clicked off so Nash couldn't argue with him about traveling all the way to Collier's Creek. And why wouldn't Xavier want to come and make sure his brother was okay?

After downloading and activating MobileTrkr, Nash added Max's number to the app. He was so nervous he had to sit down on the side of the bed. What if this didn't work? What if Max's phone ran out of battery? What if, what if.

Within seconds, a red dot appeared on his screen. It took another thirty seconds for the map to resolve. Nash used his thumb and index finger to make the map larger. For the first time in his life, he wished Wyoming wasn't quite as vast and wide open as it was. He moved the map around trying to find a landmark, anything.

"Gotcha!" He exclaimed as the closest road to the red dot appeared. *Nine Mile Road.*

"What the fuck is he doing out there?"

Not wanting to waste what remained of Max's battery life, he texted him:

This is Nash. I'm on my way.

Probably he should call JD and let him know where Max was. But Nash decided he'd ride to the rescue while Sheriff Morgan hunted down the fucker who was responsible for this fucking fucked-up situation. Of course, it was possible that the thumb drive had nothing to do with Max's disappearance, but Nash sincerely doubted it.

Nine Mile Road was, as one would expect, nine miles long. It ran along the eastern edge of Twisted Pine property, which was also a bit suspect in his mind. The land across the road from Twisted Pine had been part of one of the original silver mines Jacob Collier built but had been tapped out before the beginning of the twentieth century. He thought the county owned it now.

Nash was behind the wheel of his truck and racing through Collier's Creek, breaking pretty much every driving law in town. As he started up Bear Claw Road—the road where he'd been unforgivably rude to Max and yet Max had forgiven him anyway—he called the Sheriff's Office.

"Ben," he said before Ben could say anything more than hello, "it's Nash. I'm on my way out to Nine Mile. Max is out there." He wasn't going to explain how he knew that. Time was of the essence.

"Um, okay. I'll let Sheriff Morgan know. He's got his eye on Jake's and Deputy Kent is MIA at the moment. Oh, hang on, he's just texted me to say Deputy Kent met him at the parking lot. One of them will meet you there."

His headlights lit up the bullet hole-ridden sign for Nile Mile. Idiots with guns shot at anything, and the county rarely replaced the street signs anymore. Nash slowed just enough to take the turn without going into a ditch.

The road was paved for the first mile or so, then it turned to gravel with massive divots where 4x4s had driven after heavy rain or snowmelt. While he drove, Nash kept one eye on his phone, watching the red dot get bigger and bigger until he was as close as he could get in his truck.

Pulling to a stop, he cut the engine and jumped out. It was pitch fucking black; the truck's headlights seemed to barely make a dent in the stygian darkness. The moon had been out but was now hiding behind a thick layer of clouds that were probably carrying the snow Burl had predicted.

Leaning back into the cab, Nash grabbed the industrial flashlight out of the glove compartment. Shutting the door, he vaulted the fence and made for the tiny structure he'd seen in the distance.

"Max," he called out as he stumbled across the stone- and boulder-ridden expanse. "It's me, Nash."

There was no response, and Nash's heart was in his throat. Then he heard it, just a little louder than a whisper.

"Nash? Is that really you?"

The sound of Max's voice almost brought him to his knees.

He had to stop moving for a moment and take oxygen into his lungs.

"Oh, thank god, it's you. I was worried they were going to come back."

Max's hoarse, raspy voice was the most beautiful sound he'd ever heard.

The door was open and Nash stepped through, leading with his flashlight. The beam landed directly on Max, who squinted and turned his head to protect his eyes. He was sitting on the floor, one shoulder against the wall.

"Do you mind?"

"Sorry!" Nash lowered the flashlight but left it turned on as he hurried to his side. "Shit, Max, what the fuck happened?"

Max was a mess. He had two black eyes and his nose had obviously bled at some point because his shirt was stained. And he was filthy, covered with mud and grass and god knew what else. Nash kneeled down and gathered him in his arms like the precious person he was.

"Oh, my god, I've never been so scared in my life."

"You're telling me," Max said into Nash's shoulder. "I'd hug you back but my wrists are still handcuffed."

"Fucking hell." Nash released his hold and rose to his feet, tugging Max up along with him.

"Question," Max said as Nash looped his arm through Max's and started back toward his truck. "Can we have a do-over on the date? I'm still hungry."

"How can you joke right now?"

"I already cried, and it hurt because I'm pretty sure my nose is fractured. He punched me in the face! What did I ever do?"

"Whoever did this is going to pay," Nash promised.

"I didn't see anything," Max told him. "The first guy took me by surprise and the second guy—he came to meet the first one—I never saw at all. I could possibly identify his hairy arm, but I don't know if that's admissible."

They arrived at Nash's truck and Nash helped Max into the passenger seat.

"One second. Sit forward a bit."

Max sat up and Nash got out the wire clippers he stored in the glove compartment. Quickly, he snipped the links.

"We'll have JD or somebody take the cuffs off at the station."

"I have to say, after spending several hours in those, I no longer have any interest in exploring bondage."

Nash quirked an eyebrow. "Did you before?"

Nash wasn't really a kinky guy but if Max was interested, he wouldn't say no.

"No. Would you please kiss me—gently? So I know I'm alive and you aren't a figment of my imagination?"

Before heading to the Sheriff's Office, Nash took Max to the emergency room. There he was prescribed ibuprofen and lots of rest. The doctor declared he didn't have a concussion and confirmed his nose was fractured.

"I won't be mistaken for Xavier anymore," Max said, sounding a bit pleased. The nurse assured him his nose would, in fact, heal just fine.

"In a week or so you won't be able to tell that anything happened."

Nash was ready to get back to the motel. It was almost two in the morning, and Sheriff Morgan was finished taking Max's statement. Unfortunately, no one had shown up looking for the thumb drive at Jake's. JD had left Deputy Kent on-site for the rest of the night, just in case, and Ben had already been sent home, even though he offered to stay.

"That damn thumb drive is really all we've got to go on, and maybe it's nothing."

"I'm sorry I didn't see more or recognize either of their voices," Max said around a yawn.

"You have nothing to be sorry about, Max. You were the victim here," JD said. "Go home, clean up, and get some sleep. We'll talk more tomorrow."

"Oh shit," Nash exclaimed.

"What?"

"In all the excitement, I forgot something important." He eyed Max with something like apology. "Your brother is on his way. He'll be here by lunchtime."

"Oh my god. If my face didn't already hurt, I'd bang it on the desk. The last thing I need is Xavier showing up. He can't come."

"He's family, Max. He's your brother." Duh, Nash thought, as if Max didn't know that. "He was so concerned he called Robin before she was able to call him."

"No, I mean—whoever did this mistook me for Craig, right? I don't want Xavier showing up and something happening to him too."

JD squinted at Max and then Nash. "What exactly did they say?"

Nash listened while Max repeated the conversation the two men had before one knocked the other out.

"I'm sure they were talking about Craig. And the guy who forced me into his car lost something. The other guy told him he was going to be 'put down like a dog' and that's when he punched him."

"Did either of them say what it was? Or mention any names?"

Max shook his head. "No names. But I think he said drive. So maybe a disk drive or thumb drive? Something small enough to fit in his pocket."

Nash and JD stared at each other.

"What?" asked Max.

"Nash found a thumb drive in Jake's parking lot. Hoped it had something to do with you."

"Although I can't imagine that it does, maybe it has the guy's fingerprints on it?"

"Yeah," Nash started, "about that. I picked it up without thinking, so probably nothing on it. I was just so worried I didn't think."

"I need to call Xavier and tell him not to come."

Max had started to reach into his pocket for his freshly recharged phone when they were startled by a loud commotion coming from the lobby. Someone was shouting and hammering on the front door. JD jumped up and ran out of the room. Nash and Max looked at each other and followed JD. They'd just entered the lobby as a man stumbled inside.

"Jesus, Kent, what happened?" JD demanded, helping the man into the chair Nash had occupied earlier.

One side of Kent's face was covered with blood, and he had a napkin or paper towel pressed against his forehead. Blood from the hidden wound trickled down his cheek to his neck. He looked like something out of a zombie movie.

"Somebody caught me off guard at the parking lot," Kent said grimly. He sat back in the chair, leaning his head against the wall behind him.

"Are you kidding me?" JD exclaimed, kneeling on the floor next to Kent. "What the hell?"

"I was out of the cruiser, stretching my legs, and heard a sound. Next thing I knew, somebody came at me from behind. I turned but"—he grimaced—"they got me on the side of the head. I think I passed out for a minute. When I came to, the thumb drive was gone."

JD didn't immediately respond. Nash couldn't see the expression on his face, but his shoulders stiffened at the news. Instead, he pulled Kent's hand down so he could check the wound. The injury looked like it hurt, but Nash didn't think it was worth calling 9-1-1.

"You need me to call emergency?" JD asked, concern lacing his tone now.

"Nah." Deputy Kent shook his head, wincing as he did so. "It's just a scrape. Hurts like a motherfucker but I'll be fine."

Rising to his feet, JD left the room for a moment. When he returned, he carried a wad of bandages and some antiseptic cream.

"Let me clean it up for you. And while I'm at it, tell me everything."

Deputy Kent flicked his gaze toward Nash and Max. JD looked over his shoulder as if he'd forgotten they were there.

"Don't worry about them. I can assure you they had nothing to do with whatever happened to you."

SEVENTEEN

Max

"This place again?" Max said with a put-upon sigh as Nash pulled into the Wagon Wheel's parking lot. "I guess it's okay, as long as we're not reliving The Night Max Got So Drunk He Blacked Out."

Rolling his eyes, Nash hopped out and came around to the passenger side to help Max down.

"I promise there will be no shenanigans or alcohol. I don't want to drive back out to the ranch. It's daylight in just a few hours and JD did say he wants both of us back at the Sheriff's Office later."

"Fine," Max replied taking the hand that Nash offered. "But I pay this time."

They started toward the motel's entrance. "I can't believe that someone attacked the deputy." Max was curious what was so important that someone was willing to assault a law enforcement officer over it.

"And took the thumb drive," Nash reminded him.

"That's a bummer."

Nash shot him a look.

"What?"

"JD had Ben copy the drive. The original may be gone, but they still have all the data that was on it."

"Huh, he didn't tell the deputy that."

"He sure didn't."

"Huh," Max said again.

"Huh, indeed," agreed Nash as he held the motel's lobby door open for Max.

Max halted in his steps as a thought struck him. *Xavier.* As much as he didn't want to talk to his brother tonight, he also didn't want him showing up tomorrow and walking straight into trouble.

"What?" Nash asked.

"I have to call Xavier—before he gets on that plane."

Regardless of the ridiculous hour, Xavier picked up immediately. "What?"

"Did nothing Mom taught you take hold?" Max complained. "*What* is not how you answer a phone call."

"*What* is a fine way to answer the phone when my brother has been abducted by some creepy fucker and dragged out into a corn field."

"It wasn't a corn field. It was more just grass and rocks."

"Are you arguing with me about what type of field a murderer took you to? The Autobiography of Maxmillian Stone, who was killed in a field of grass, not corn." Max knew Xavier was trying to be funny, but he sounded angry and scared.

"Xavier, I'm fine. A few bumps and bruises, but Nash found me in time—thanks to you—and now I'm back at the motel and ready to go to bed. Don't fly out here. There's nothing you can do, and you know you hate flying over the Cascades."

There was a silence and a shuffling sound. "Lebowski, we've talked about this. The bed just isn't big enough."

Lebowski was Xavier's golden retriever rescue. Max hadn't met him in person yet, but Xavier constantly sent selfies of himself and the dog.

"Besides, who will watch the dog?"

"Mom, duh."

As if Wanda didn't have two needy rescues of her own to take care of.

"But," Xavier said, "if you're sure about not coming out, I'll cancel the flight. I really do hate flying over the mountains."

"I'm sure. I'm fine. I'm also tired and want to go to sleep now." Max flopped down on the bed, hardly able to keep his eyes open.

"Is that sexy cowboy going to keep watch over you?"

Max caught Nash's amused grin. Xavier was not a quiet talker, but maybe he was speaking loudly on purpose this time.

Nash crossed over to where Max lay on his back. "You can bet on it, Xavier. Max is safe with me. I plan on taking care of him for as long as he'll let me."

Max could almost hear Xavier rolling his eyes. "Alright, I guess he's okay then. Don't do anything I wouldn't do."

It was Max's turn to snort. "That leaves me a lot of possibilities, Xav."

"Fuck off. I'm going back to sleep. Love you, brother."

"Love you too."

Max came awake much faster than he would've liked to. Unlike the last time he'd stayed at the Wagon Wheel, he immediately remembered why he felt like he'd been hit by a train.

"Fucking hell."

The mattress dipped and Nash was leaning over him.

"Can I get you anything? Painkillers? Water?"

He went through a mental checklist of his body's complaints.

"Coffee before I die of lack of caffeine. Then ibuprofen. What time is it?"

Nash rolled over to check. Good thing, since Max wasn't sure he could manage it.

"Shit, it's later than I thought. Almost ten. I bet JD is champing at the bit to talk to you."

"Ugh." Max stared up at the wood beam ceiling. "I need all the pain relievers, a vat of coffee, and some clothes that don't look like I was assaulted and kidnapped."

"You were assaulted and kidnapped," Nash pointed out.

Max nodded. It hurt his head. "Yes, but I'd rather not everyone in Collier's Creek think this is my normal."

Nash chuckled. "Maybe this is your new normal. Mild-mannered software executive changing things up. Chinos and button-downs during the day but at night, all bets are off. What will it be today? Spin the wheel and find out."

"Would you *please* stop being ridiculous—it hurts to laugh—and bring me the coffee and meds you offered?"

Snorting quietly, Nash flipped the covers back and got out of bed, heading for the dresser and the bottle of pills. Funny, it didn't hurt when Max turned his head to watch Nash cross the room.

"I was thinking about what you told me was on the thumb drive."

"Yeah?"

He watched as Nash, wearing only a pair of black boxer briefs, flicked on the room's coffee maker. The brew was guaranteed to be horrible, but it was a start. On the other hand, he got to ogle Nash's trim body. Maybe he wasn't as sore as he'd thought.

Right, he'd been thinking. "The names you mentioned. Little Wind, Shoshone, et cetera. In Washington, the legal casinos are tribal. I don't know about Little Wind but Shoshone is a tribe here, right?"

Nash nodded as he padded back to sit on the edge of the bed.

"Little Wind is a casino, and so is Shoshone."

"I bet"—Max snickered at his unintended pun—"the other names have something to do with casinos or gambling. I don't remember a lot from that time, but I do remember my mom fighting with Craig about spending hours at bars playing pull tabs. I wouldn't be surprised if he had a gambling addiction. I know this is a stretch, but I just couldn't turn my brain off last night."

"Keep going," Nash encouraged. "I think you could be onto something. The other names are towns where some of the biggest rodeos in Wyoming—hell, the US—are held."

"People bet on those too?"

"You bet your sweet ass they do."

"So." Max struggled to pull himself up higher on his pillows. "Craig Stone got himself deep into debt. Maybe he's always been but"—he waved a hand—"that doesn't matter. He was in bad trouble. No way did he gamble legally. And finally, some crooked bookie got tired of it and wanted the money Craig owed them."

Standing up, Nash began to pace the room, his fingers laced together on the top of his head as he appeared to think, and then he spoke. "This is good, Max. It's the only way it makes sense that he would ask Robin for money. I mean seriously, it had to be a last resort. But the ranch is broke. So then what?"

Max was trying to avoid looking at the lurid painting in this room, but again, it was impossible. This mural was possibly a depiction of the Lewis and Clark Expedition. Had they come through Wyoming? Sacajawea looked pissed off and prepared to push the explorers over a rocky cliff into a raging river while Clark or Lewis appeared to be mansplaining. Some things never changed.

"Earth to Max."

"Right, sorry." He waved a hand toward the walls in explanation. "I was distracted. Then the bad guys make good on their threat, but they saw me and thought I was Craig, which is not out of the realm of possibility. Then whoever it is kills the real Craig, but they're already freaked out because they tried to kill the wrong person the first time. How would they know Craig had sons that look like him?"

Max paused and considered the man who'd attacked him in Jake's. He'd definitely seemed surprised, shocked even.

"The guy in the hallway said, 'You again,' like he was surprised to see me. I think he panicked. The second guy was pissed off when he arrived."

"But we still don't know who they are," Nash pointed out, swinging back around to face Max. Those briefs were very distracting. Maybe they should leave crime-solving to the sheriff and just stay in bed all day.

The coffee maker sputtered and hissed in the ensuing silence as the last of the water pushed through the heater. Nash dropped his hands and moved across to the dresser, turning the tiny cups over so he could fill them up. Shaking a couple of Advil into one hand, he brought them to Max along with a cup of coffee.

"I love you," Max blurted as he watched him. Dammit, he'd meant to be much cooler about how he felt. Now his cheeks burned with thermo-nuclear intensity, but Max forced himself to continue. "Last night, I... Well, actually, I've known for a while now but was afraid to say anything. But if I'd died last night... anyway, I wanted to say the words out loud. To you. I love you, Nash Vigil."

Max cringed inwardly, wishing he had the ability to become invisible. He didn't though and was just going to have to deal with the fallout of his words. With a gentle smile, Nash held the pain pills out to him but set the coffee cup on the nightstand. Then he sat on the edge of the bed, the mattress dipping under his weight, causing Max to shift toward him. Max's heart was beating so fast he felt faint. And so embarrassed. He'd never realized falling in love would be so damn awkward.

"I love you too, Max Stone."

Max almost asked him to repeat himself. Had Nash just said he loved him? For real?

"I want to take you to the ocean," Max blurted. "I want to be there when you see it for the first time. I want to share my life with you."

Would this verbal diarrhea never stop? Was he cursed to open his mouth and have every private thought just dribble out? He'd started to slide down the sheet and pushed himself back up. In for a penny, in for a pound.

"A house, goats, horses, a dog or two. But goats are the only kids I want. Maybe. I want everything. With you. I can live anywhere—and anywhere seems to be Wyoming. I will never ask you to leave Twisted Pine. There's acreage for sale not far from the ranch. We could build our own house—"

Nash leaned in, pressing his lips against Max's. Slowly, gently, he pushed Max backward into his pillows. His lips parted and Nash's tongue swept in tangling with Max's. How long they kissed like this, Max couldn't gauge. Max grunted a protest when Nash pulled away. His lips were puffy and slick, giving Max other ideas.

"Max, I love you too. I know you're a carer, a problem solver. So am I. But we don't have to figure everything out today. Or even in the next few days. We can take things as they come, right? Can you trust that I love you too?"

"And you'll let me take you to the ocean?" Max felt this was very important.

"Yes, I will go to the ocean with you. But you have to get back up on Buttercup. I'm going to make a cowboy out of you."

"Can't I just make out *with* a cowboy?"

Nash shot him a sexy grin. "Just this cowboy."

Then he leaned close again, licking across Max's lips and—carefully—tucking into his side.

Their coffee was cold by the time they came up for air, interrupted by the ring of Nash's cell phone and an urgent summons to the Sheriff's Office.

Sheriff Morgan slid a photo across his desk. "Any chance you recognize this man?"

Max looked down at what was very clearly a picture of a dead person. JD looked exhausted and Max wondered if he'd slept since they'd last seen him. The corpse had dark hair, heavy jowls, and a distinctive nose. It had obviously been broken more than once. There was also a bullet hole in his forehead.

"Is this the man who attacked me?" he asked.

The sheriff shrugged. "He was found this morning, not long after you two left."

"Where?" asked Nash.

"The fairgrounds, or close enough."

"Who is it?" Max stared at the picture, doing his best to recognize him. Was he the man from Jake's? Max just couldn't be sure; the few glimpses he'd gotten of his captor added up to not much.

"Not sure. There was no ID with the body."

"So why are you showing us the picture?" Nash wanted to know.

JD sat back in his chair, and it squeaked. The sheriff grimaced and shifted his weight a bit before answering.

"We found the thumb drive in his pocket."

Not what Max had been expecting to hear. Although maybe he should've, seeing as the sheriff had wanted to see them immediately.

"We were hoping you could ID him as your attacker. Having the thumb drive doesn't mean he's the one, but it's strong evidence. Luckily, he was in the system, so fingerprints ID'd him for us. Does the name Norman Quail mean anything to you?"

Max shook his head. Nash did too.

"Quail was a small-time collections man."

"What does this mean?" Max asked. "That he's been killed? Nash and I think that Craig was up to his ears in gambling debt. He had a history—although I'd have to ask my mom for more details and I'd rather not."

JD looked Max in the eye. "While hope is not a word I like to toss around. I am hopeful that this means you are no longer in danger. Especially with Stone already dead."

Taking turns, Max and Nash shared the theory they'd come up with that morning about Craig Stone's possible gambling debts and why Max may have been targeted.

"I look a lot like my dad—I can see someone mistaking me for him from afar."

JD nodded. "Judging by Quail's rap sheet, I wouldn't be surprised if you're on to something. He didn't appear to have been the sharpest tool in the shed, and it does seem that you are out of danger. Still, I want you to be extra vigilant. We don't know who killed Quail. It may have nothing to do with all this, but the fact that he had the drive tells me otherwise."

"I'll be careful," Max assured the Sheriff.

Nash's hand landed on Max's thigh. "I'll keep him safe, JD."

EPILOGUE

Epilogue

"Keep the blindfold over your eyes," Max instructed. "No peeking."

"This is ridiculous. I've seen pictures of the ocean, just not the real thing."

"Well, the real thing is totally different. No cheating."

Max felt the tiniest bit bad about the blindfold since he'd made Nash put it on as they passed Elma. They were close now though, having already passed the Forest Service buildings and the Cooper Springs Police Station.

"Just another few minutes. I'm going to park at the resort."

He'd rented a cabin there for them too. No way were he and Nash staying with his mother and her boyfriend, or with Xavier and his boyfriend and his boyfriend's daughter. He was planning on buying his own property here. Max loved Wyoming but found he missed the foggy Washington coast days, the emerald-green mosses and—shockingly—the rain.

The single stop light in town was green, which seemed like

some kind of sign, and on the right was the drive into Cooper Springs Resort. Flicking the blinker, he turned in.

The day was perfect, hardly a cloud in the blue sky over their heads and just a light breeze coming off the water.

"Wait there."

"Oh my god, you are bossy."

Nash's stomach rumbled loud enough to be heard over the engine.

Max didn't bother replying to the accusation of bossiness. They both knew who was bossy in their relationship, and it wasn't Max. Coming around the front of his car, Max opened the passenger door and helped Nash out.

"Just trust me. When we're done here, I'll take you to the pub for something to eat."

He just knew Nash was rolling his eyes under the thin fabric —he could practically hear them—as he grasped his arm and started to lead him down the marsh trail to the beach. They should've stopped in Aberdeen for a snack, but Max had been too excited about finally getting Nash to the Washington coast.

"There's a little bridge here we're going to cross," Max warned, "and then it's another fifty yards or so."

Above them circled seagulls and a few crows, coasting along on the wind looking for their dinner. Or, in the crows' cases, possibly just playing on the drafts. Max drew the sea air deep into his lungs. He'd learned to love the scent of hay and grasses around Twisted Pine, the smell of pine needles when the temperatures were high, but the smell of the sea was embedded in his genes.

This was the first time Max had been back to Cooper Springs since last fall. He and Nash had spent the winter and spring negotiating where and how much house they wanted to build. Nash'd had this idea that things needed to be fifty-fifty, which was noble but sort of ridiculous considering the balance in Max's bank account. A few months ago, Max had sat his cowboy down and after a vigorous argument and incredible make-up sex, he'd convinced Nash to let Max build the house of their dreams.

If Robin was willing to let Max help her—and she had been, so the worst of the loans were paid off, giving Twisted Pine some much-needed breathing room—then Nash needed to let Max's software money pay for a house. And land. And a few rescue horses that Nash had brought home to Twisted Pine. Privately, Max thought it was the idea of being able to save abandoned horses that brought Nash to his way of thinking, but it had worked.

"Seriously, are we there yet?" Nash sounded a great deal like a petulant four-year-old.

Max snickered. He'd stopped walking at the edge of the beach where the sand started, leaving Nash standing there with his blindfold on. Reaching over, he tugged the fabric away.

"Ta-dah!"

Instead of looking out at the glittering water, Max was watching Nash's handsome face as he got his first up-close look of the Pacific Ocean.

His cowboy was silent for several minutes, then he started to step out onto the sand.

"Wait, take your boots off."

Max waved him over to a beach log that had rolled up in a fierce storm when he was in high school. Sitting down, Nash pulled off his boots and socks, and Max followed suit. Standing again with the sand tickling his toes, Max offered Nash his hand.

Together, they walked out onto the beach. A few people meandered along the waterline. Some under-fives were playing in tide pools revealed by the retreating water, supervised by parents or perhaps older siblings.

"This is fucking incredible. It's huge, it's vast, it's more than I ever imagined," Nash finally said, his voice barely audible over the sound of the surf. "I love you so much. Thank you for bringing me here."

"Wait until family dinner night, then maybe you'll change mind. Which is tomorrow, by the way."

Nash swung around to face him. "Yeah, no, you can't scare me with family dinner night. Unfortunately for you, you're stuck with me." He stepped all the way into Max's space, his chest brushing against Max's. There was some emotion in his eyes that Max couldn't parse.

"I'm afraid this means—" Nash paused, dropping to one knee on the sand in front of him. Max's heart jumped to his throat. What was happening? "I need to make an honest man out of you, whatever that means." He glanced up at Max, his blue eyes sparking in the bright afternoon sunlight. "Maximillian Stone, will you do me the honor of marrying me?"

Max's mouth opened shut and opened again. Nash's image blurred for some reason, but then he blinked and Nash came back into focus.

"Are you going to keep me hanging down here?" Nash asked.

"Yes, I will marry you." Max nodded, hard, in case just a yes wasn't enough for his cowboy.

Nash stood up and stuck his hand into his jeans pocket, pulling out a small velvet bag. Opening it, he shook a pair of bands into his palm.

"Hold out your hand."

Complying, Max watched as Nash picked out one of the rings and gently slipped it on to Max's finger. It fit him perfectly. Like it was meant to be there. He stared at his hand and the weighty ring, the only thing keeping him from floating away.

"Phew, I had to guess your size."

What was he thinking? It was Nash, practical Nash Vigil, who tethered him. The rings were just a symbol. They were simple, just plain yellow gold. Which pleased Max. He couldn't imagine Nash wearing something fancy.

"Let me put yours on." Max held his hand out.

Nash dropped the other ring onto Max's palm. Carefully, his

fingers trembling, Max picked it up and slipped the band onto Nash's finger.

"I didn't know it would feel this way," Nash muttered, staring at the gold encircling his finger.

"What way?"

"Like the best choice I've ever made."

∿

Read Sheriff of the Creek next! A grumpy-sunshine romance from Sue Brown.

A grumpy, small-town sheriff loves his dispatcher with the heart of sunshine. And no one is ever going to find out, especially the man he loves. Then danger rolls into town. Will the sheriff step up and protect his love?

If you started with Mandatory Repairs don't miss, The Best Kind of Awkward by Becca Seymour. Small-town single dad, yum!

∿

Curious about Max's brother Xavier? He gets his story in Adverse Conditions the first in my Reclaimed Hearts series! Check out the cover so you know how sexy Maximillian is—how could Nash resist?

∿

Join the highway to Elle newsletter for a free short story set in Xavier and Vincent's past... NSFW. Set at the end of high school. Just click here: The Incident.

THANK YOU FROM ELLE

Thank you for reading my book, seriously.

If you enjoyed *Mandatory Repairs*, I would greatly appreciate if you would let your friends know so they can experience Max, Nash and the gang at Twisted Pine ranch As with all of my books, I have enabled lending on all platforms in which it is allowed to make it easy to share with a friend. If you leave a review for Mandatory Repairs or any of my books, on the site from which you purchased the book, Goodreads, Bookbub, or your own blog, I would love to read it! Email me the link at elle@ellekeaton.com

Keep up-to-date with new releases and sales, *The Highway to Elle* hits your in-box approximately every two weeks, sometimes more sometimes less. I include deals, freebies and new releases as well as a sort of rambling running commentary on what *this* author's life is like. I'd love to have you aboard! I also have a Facebook reader group called the Highway to Elle, come say hi!

ABOUT ELLE

Do you love inclusive, swoony, and often suspenseful small-town romances featuring complex characters and a unique sense of place? I do too! My characters start out broken and, *maybe*, they're still a tad banged up by the end, but they find the other half of their hearts and ALWAYS get their happily ever after.

In 2017 I pressed the Publish button for the first time and have never looked back—making this the longest period of time I've stuck with a job in my entire life.

Currently, there are over thirty Elle Keaton books available for you to read or listen to. I love cats and dogs. Star Wars and Star Trek. Pineapple on pizza, and have a cribbage habit my husband encourages.

Connecting with readers is very important to me. If you are so inclined, join The Highway to Elle newsletter, and keep up to date with everything Elle-related (or join my Ream page and get in on the novels early plus swag and extras). Random topics Include, but not limited to, 'where are Elle's glasses?' and, 'why are there cats?'. I can also be found on Facebook, Instagram, and occasionally TikTok.

Series:

Shielded Hearts M/M romantic suspense

Veiled Intentions M/M romantic suspense - same couple

West Coast Forensics - M/M romantic suspense - different couples

Reclaimed Hearts - Mystery and Suspense adjacent

Home in Hollyridge - small town contemporary MM romance

Printed in Great Britain
by Amazon

33314721R00098